"You may now kiss

Vasili heard the words. The and dreaded was upon him. For two weeks he had wanted to kiss her. Images of her against the door of his office flashed in his mind once again. He had wanted a taste of her then, and after replaying that moment so frequently, he wasn't sure that he would want to stop once his lips met hers. So, with her hands still in his, Vasili mustered every bit of control he had and leaned in, placing a chaste kiss upon her lips, but as if it were a trap designed just for him, this one simple touch caused the very air to snap around them.

He was utterly lost to the current that swept them both away and it was only the sound of polite clapping and an amused chuckle close by that broke through the haze, wrenching him back.

With careful tenderness he pulled away, noticing the look in Helia's eyes. Like a raging sea. He knew she was just as affected as he was.

Maybe there was an upside to this marriage after all.

Bella Mason has been a bookworm from an early age. She has been regaling people with stories from the time she discovered she could hold the dinner table hostage with her reimagined fairy tales. After earning a degree in journalism, she rekindled her love of writing and she now writes full-time. When she isn't imagining dashing heroes and strong heroines, she can be found exploring Melbourne, with her nose in a book or lusting after fast cars.

Also by Bella Mason

Harlequin Presents

Awakened by the Wild Billionaire
Secretly Pregnant by the Tycoon
Their Diamond Ring Ruse

Visit the Author Profile page
at Harlequin.com.

His Chosen Queen

BELLA MASON

PRESENTS

Recycling programs
for this product may
not exist in your area.

ISBN-13: 978-1-335-59356-6

His Chosen Queen

Harlequin Enterprises ULC
22 Adelaide St. West, 41st Floor
Toronto, Ontario M5H 4E3, Canada
www.Harlequin.com

Printed in Lithuania

His Chosen Queen

For Brad, without whom none of my books would ever have been written.

In you, I have found my king.

CHAPTER ONE

IT WAS REMARKABLE how some days could seem completely ordinary. How the sun would beat down as it always did, how the sounds in the air didn't change, how people could go about their lives as normal and yet everything could be different. Changed.

Prince Vasili Leos, 'spare' to the throne of the small Mediterranean island kingdom of Thalonia, located in the Ionian Sea, sat in the darkened office of the private secretary to the King. He'd never liked this office, and would try to avoid it at all costs. The wood-panelled walls and polished wood floors were suffocating. It wasn't a room to make anyone feel at ease, and ease was the last thing on his mind now.

Only the barest hints of sunlight passed through the slats of the dark wooden blinds, landing in penumbral stripes on the highly polished desk that was devoid of all clutter. And in the centre of all that light and dark, as if a divine spotlight was cast upon it, sat a letter with his name on it. A letter that currently consumed his existence. A letter that he wouldn't have had if it hadn't been for the news that had broken his world apart.

The King of Thalonia was dead.

Vasili was now King.

His brother Leander had been flying over the mainland when his plane had crashed. There were no survivors.

The King's private secretary, Andreas Kyriakou, was speaking, but Vasili barely heard a word.

He was numb. Mere hours ago he had been sharing a drink with his brother, the rightful King, and now he was gone. An entire life wiped out. His only real family. And now he sat in this uncomfortable chair, hardly feeling the carved wood his arms rested on, to be told they had to move on swiftly.

Vasili had never wanted to be King. He was the spare. The insurance policy. The 'Playboy Prince', as he had been dubbed. He had never been intended for the throne and he didn't want it.

'Your Majesty, are you listening?' Andreas asked, halting his pacing.

No, Vasili wasn't listening. He didn't want to. Everything was happening so fast it was a blur. The sun was still low in the sky. The morning had barely begun. And in that time he had been summoned to Andreas's office and, without any preamble at all, had been told his brother was dead. Now, without waiting or caring about how that news had landed, they had already read Leander's will. The letter had been left in his brother's care to be given to Vasili in the event of his death.

Vasili glared at the white envelope. He shouldn't have received it. Not yet, at least.

'We need you to take the throne immediately. You need to speak to the people. Make sure they know the monarchy stands strong.'

Vasili curled his fingers into fists. He was still trying to process the fact that his brother was gone and all Andreas could do was talk of his ascension. Still, he remained silent. In this void he had landed in the thrum of his steady heart could be felt throughout his body. All he could see was that letter. A physical representation of the fact that Leander was gone and that Thalonia was now looking at a twenty-nine-year-old king in the seat of power. It was ridiculous. Just as ridiculous as the fact that yet another letter had been left to him by his father. A man who had shown him nothing but disapproval. The rebellious son…

The first had been after his death, barely a year ago, but Vasili had had no interest in what his father had had to say. In anger, he had immediately tossed that letter into the fireplace, and he had no inclination to open this letter either. He didn't know if he ever wanted to read it. The contents could stay buried for all he cared. Just like the man himself.

His illness had come on swiftly, and before they'd known it the Kingdom had been plunged into mourning and Leander had ascended the throne. A role he had trained for his whole life. A role never meant for Vasili. One that the more superstitious of his people had come to believe was cursed.

And now allaying their fears would have to fall to him. It had to be some sort of cosmic joke! His people would once again sink into a pit of mourning and he couldn't blame them. Leander had been a popular king and, given the fact that only Andreas was in this office with him, Vasili surmised that Carissa, their communications secretary, was making the announcement to the people as they spoke.

'Thalonia requires stability, Your Maj—'

Vasili cut Andreas a glare that had him falling silent. He rounded the desk, sitting in the overlarge chair behind it.

'Your Majesty, I understand that you do not wish to hear this, but I will say it again. Thalonia requires stability and it is your responsibility. This is your duty.'

Vasili wanted to laugh, but there wasn't an ounce of humour within him. All there was were jumbled thoughts, and at the forefront of all of that was this blasted letter.

He could not fathom why his father would have left it to him for this moment. Throughout his entire life neither his father nor his mother had had any time for him at all. He was the spare. His existence merely a tick-box exercise. Why would they care about him when Leander has been the son who would one day lead the nation. They were King and Queen after all. Their time had been much too precious to be spent frivolously.

So what could the great Athanasios Leos have to say to him now? If he couldn't even invest the barest hint of time in his youngest son when he'd needed him, what could he say now when he didn't? Had he not been the one who had warned Vasili not to waste Leander's time as a child? And yet here he was being asked to rescue the very institution for which he had never been good enough.

In fact, the only person who had been there for him as he'd grown up had been his nanny. The palace had employed several royal nannies, but only one had ever tended to him. She had raised him. Had given him the support and love he had missed so badly from his parents. She had been the only person he'd known he could count on, but when he had turned fifteen she had been let go, and that was when he'd known without a shadow of a doubt that whatever he wanted or cared for meant little to the crown.

So he had swallowed down his grief and decided that the crown meant nothing to him either. Resentment and rebellion had been born bright in him. He didn't care about the throne. He didn't care about being a prince. If he was of so little value, then all his family stood for held little value for him. And so he'd become the 'Playboy Prince', with no interest in ruling. It had seemed to be what aggravated his parents the most, so Vasili had freely indulged himself in his hedonistic lifestyle.

Rebellion had suited him well. Especially when all his parents had focused on was the monarchy and Leander.

Vasili had understood that. He'd understood the dedication that ruling a kingdom required. He'd even understood the attention Leander received. He was meant to be King. What he hadn't understood was why those things had made his life void.

At least none of it had affected his relationship with his brother. Vasili had often been ordered to refrain from distracting his brother, and he'd obeyed, but that hadn't stopped Leander from sneaking into Vasili's room at night. From the time he was little they would share pilfered treats from the kitchens, until they'd grown older, when they had shared a drink.

While they hadn't been able to be as close as siblings ought to be, or even really friends, Vasili had still looked up to his brother. Admired him even in adulthood. And now he was gone. Without a warning or a goodbye. He would never see Leander again. His brother was dead and what was he left with? An advisor he could barely tolerate and a kingdom that would be disappointed.

Vasili closed his eyes for a breath, the reality of the situation crashing upon him. With his mother having long since passed, and having buried his father only a year ago, now losing Leander meant he was alone. Completely alone.

This palace, grand and ostentatious, with its Rococo architecture, was the jewel of Seidon—Thalonia's popular capital—and had been home to generations of his family and a battalion of staff, and never once had it felt quite so empty.

Of course Vasili had friends. An entire network of them.

People who loved to party as much as him. Who were after a good time. And not a single one of them could he call now. Not one could he lean on or go to for support. He couldn't think of what he would say in any case. Love and support were alien concepts to him, having never had the privilege of experiencing it for himself. So he would have to deal with this, with his immense grief, as he dealt with everything else in his life. Alone.

'Your Majesty,' Andreas said more forcefully. If he was at all aware of Vasili's spiralling thoughts he didn't show it. 'You are now King. This is something you must accept. We have to move immediately. Thalonia cannot be without its king.'

Vasili was aware of that, and yet Andreas's constant badgering had lit the wick of his anger. He needed a moment— one moment to himself. Alone. A moment to say goodbye to his brother and steel himself for whatever was to come.

'And, furthermore, we need to move quickly to secure the future of the crown. You need to settle on an adequate bride and you need to marry and produce heirs as soon as possible. It is imperative—'

'Enough!' Vasili spat angrily, pushing to his feet and silencing Andreas.

He had heard just about as much as he could take from the older man. Swiping the letter off the table, Vasili strode out of the gloomy office, slamming the door shut behind him.

His angry footsteps echoed through the marble hallways of the palace, and a swirling cloud of fury and grief consumed Vasili as he tried to put as much space between him and Andreas as possible. Because right now it would take nothing for the tether on his temper to snap entirely.

Sensing his dark mood, the palace staff kept their eyes

low and gave him a wide berth as they continued with their day. Vasili wondered if they already knew Leander was dead. They had to have been informed, and yet none offered him even hollow words of sympathy.

Seeking solitude, Vasili was grateful, but wouldn't show it.

There was only one place he could go where he would find the peace he was after. The library. The silence there would be welcome.

He pushed open the gilded door and stepped into the grandest library in all the Kingdom. It was a cavernous two-storey space, with rows upon rows of shelves, every single one packed with books of every colour and topic. Branching off the main space, with its gleaming marble floors, were passages to rooms and alcoves looking out over the palace gardens, where there were even more books. Frescoes in shades of pastel blue and pink covered the ceiling, drawing the eye up the gold-accented white walls.

There weren't too many things Vasili was grateful to his forebears for, but this place was one. Even though he had rarely stepped into the library in the last few years, the colours in here always reminded him of the island itself. Of early mornings when the sky was painted in pink and blue with streaks of gold. When the turquoise waters were a siren's call to all who looked upon them. White clouds in the sky and sand on the beach.

Except today he didn't revel in all the ways he enjoyed this place. Today he just found a seat in a comfortable chair in a quiet corner and closed his eyes.

He prayed for just a little peace. His brother had died. He hadn't been told if there was a body to recover. He hadn't even gone back to his brother's room to whisper a quiet goodbye. He was already being forced to move on.

This entire institution was heartless. He had learned that at fifteen, but it seemed he was having to learn the lesson all over again.

Vasili was thankful that it was quiet. It was still early enough that the library was completely empty. He had no idea where the librarian was—was just happy that whoever it was had left him be.

But this was a day that was meant to test him, and what little peace he had hoped to get was shattered when the library doors were thrown open and in walked Andreas, followed by the communications secretary, Carissa.

Vasili groaned. His temper frayed further.

'Your Majesty,' Andreas said, dripping disapproval.

The man had served his father and brother, and was clearly unhappy that the crown would now fall to him. Vasili could see it.

'You cannot simply walk away from this.'

'Please, Your Majesty…' Carissa tried a different tack.

A tall woman with straw-light hair, cut sharply along her jaw, impeccably clad in a dark tailored suit, she took the chair angled towards his and spoke to him in a tone he assumed must work wonders in getting anyone to do as she bid. But no amount of charm or authority would work on him. Not now.

'Just listen,' she said. 'And then we can decide on a way forward that works for everyone.'

Vasili huffed. 'For everyone?'

'Of course, sir. We're in a tough situation and we all want to do what's best,' Carissa said.

'She's right,' a still-scowling Andreas agreed. 'It's imperative that you listen to us. You have to marry and produce heirs. King Leander didn't do so quickly enough, and now the crown sits in a precarious position.'

Vasili tilted his head, studying the private secretary. 'Let me guess…it's my duty to save the monarchy?'

'Of course it is. Thalonia needs its king,' Andreas replied.

Vasili shook his head. Saving the system he had rebelled against his whole life—the very thing responsible for him being cast aside—was the last thing he wanted to do.

He was sorely tempted to let it all fall to ruin. One family didn't make an entire kingdom. Besides, he hadn't been enough at any point in his life before, so why should he be now? Vasili believed he was the very last person who should ever marry. He didn't want marriage. Commitment wasn't something he had ever considered. He much preferred losing himself in a beautiful woman who understood his needs. Knew that it was only for a night. That there would never be a future with him.

He was trying to escape the cage, not invite others to join him in it.

His mother had once called him a Lothario and Vasili would much rather wear that title than the title of King.

'Clearly not just a king,' Vasili all but growled.

Carissa cut Andreas off before he could utter whatever was brewing on his tongue. 'We understand your trepidation, sir—'

'I doubt that.'

She continued as if the new King had not interrupted her. 'But we are here to help you take on this task. You can lean on us, and we can guide you through these changes.'

How weak did these people think he was? With their pretty words that blatantly told him they would try to control him.

'And one such change is your lifestyle,' Andreas chipped in. 'Not just because it is unbecoming behaviour for the

King, but because it would also be highly inappropriate when you wed.'

When? It had gone from something Vasili *should* do to an inevitability. As if his choices, his life, didn't matter.

'We can help you find an appropriate bride.'

'What?'

Fire exploded in his veins. Andreas's eyes widened at his low, icy tone. Anger burned through his grief, igniting every rebellious urge he had ever had. He wouldn't be controlled. Wouldn't be dictated to. If the old King and Queen hadn't been able to control him, what made these people think that they could?

Marriage and children had never been on his radar, but if they wanted him to get married so badly it wouldn't be to someone they deemed 'appropriate'. Some generic royal who would be as selfish and self-obsessed as all the rest. No. He would do things on his own terms, exactly as he lived his life. Vasili couldn't care less what Andreas and Carissa wanted. To him they represented all that was wrong with the entire institution of royalty.

Feeling every bit the recalcitrant prince he was known to be, Vasili once again rebelled against the system that he could never escape. He looked over their heads, defiance etched in every line on his face, and with teeth bared he ground out, 'Fine. I'll marry *her*.'

Both royal secretaries turned around in unison, to glance in the direction of the new King's gaze, and found the librarian staring wide-eyed at the three of them, clearly having overheard the entire conversation.

'Your Majesty…' Andreas whipped back around, his face a mix of horror and frustration. 'You can't be serious.'

'Andreas is right. You can't marry the librarian. She

isn't an appropriate queen for the Kingdom,' Carissa tried to reason with him.

Vasili stared hard at the communications secretary. 'And just who would be an appropriate queen, exactly?'

'You need to marry a noble. It's tradition. Every consort in our history has been a royal in their own right. It projects the right image. Of strength and endurance. Please, you have to think of the throne.'

Carissa's words were like kindling to flame. And the realisation that she had said the wrong thing was soon reflected in her eyes.

'Are you questioning your king?' Vasili challenged.

He didn't have to raise his voice or stand over these two people he had quite honestly had enough of for one day. If he was now King, then they would see the kind of king he would be. Not one easily controlled or cowed.

Andreas looked horror-struck, as if the insinuation was the greatest insult. 'Of course not. We would never second-guess the King. But it is my job to act as his closest advisor. I have done so for your father and your brother, and as such I have to say that this is not the best course of action. King Leander was to have married a princess in two weeks.'

'Well, it seems that I need to remind you that I am not Leander. Nor will I ever be. It's best that you heed that very important fact, Andreas,' Vasili said smoothly.

'Be that as it may, sir, she is a librarian.' A puce tinge coloured his neck. 'She may work at the palace, but she is a commoner, and never in the rich history of this kingdom has a commoner ever sat on the throne. Need I remind you of our heritage? Thalonia was named after Thalia, Queen Consort of the first King. A princess before that.'

'Firstly, Andreas, I would mind my tone if I were you.' Vasili rose gracefully from his chair to stand towering above Andreas and Carissa, who hastily got to her feet to show respect. 'And secondly, there is a first time for everything. Your king has spoken.'

Vasili turned towards the librarian, still frozen at the counter. His eyes locked with hers. An arresting shade of turquoise, they widened in shock. Her heart must be beating a frantic tattoo—he could see the flutter of the pulse in her neck—but in that moment the world stood still. All that existed was him and her and nothing else.

A beat passed.

Maybe two.

Maybe an entire eon.

Then Vasili ripped his gaze away from hers and with his jaw clenched tightly, strode out of the library.

Helia tracked his movement, still rooted to the spot.

Her eyes were still locked on the door through which the new King had vanished.

'What…?' She whispered to herself in utter shock, her heart pounding furiously.

He couldn't be serious! He had no idea who she was. Marry her? The utter insanity!

Yet her heart still beat frantically, its rhythm changing, thudding, as she remembered his eyes on her. He had never looked her way before, but in that moment Helia had felt as though he was looking into her soul. As if he could see the very essence of her. Those golden-brown eyes had been a trap. Ensnaring her. And for a heartbeat she would have given up her every secret to that look. It had excited her.

Which was an immensely ludicrous thought, even though it was one she wished were true. No one went from seeing a person for the first time—a person they had never noticed before—to choosing to marry them.

Prince Vasili was grieving. He had only just found out his brother was dead—from what she had overheard—so no one could possibly take him seriously. Could they? Of course, not. His advisors would probably rush after him and that would be that.

Helia thought back to when her father had died. Grief had clouded her every thought and she had only been a teen-ager back then. Surely Andreas would see that the King was not thinking straight. The King would need a moment to collect his thoughts and then he would speak to his advisors calmly and this whole crazy interaction would be forgotten.

She would be forgotten.

Whatever hope she'd had of him having seen her flared and died with that one logical thought—but at least she would have the memory of the one time King Vasili had seen her and how good it had felt.

CHAPTER TWO

Unfortunately, given the looks on the advisors' faces, that seemed unlikely.

Andreas and Carissa approached Helia with grave expressions.

'Come with us,' Andreas instructed. 'Quietly. We need to discuss this in private.'

Helia still couldn't believe the words that had left the new King's mouth. She couldn't think that anyone would.

'Is this really necessary?' she asked.

'Yes.'

Something like hope fluttered in her belly, because that would mean Vasili really had taken notice of her. So she followed Andreas and Carissa through the palace to the private secretary's office. Not once did her heart steady its rhythm. Helia couldn't wrap her head around how her ordinary day had turned into this circus, all because the King had looked her way in a moment of madness.

'Take a seat,' Andreas instructed. 'Wait here, we'll be back shortly.' He left the room, with Carissa at his side, and closed the door.

Helia was left alone in the unwelcoming office. She could hear agitated voices beyond the door, but couldn't make out what was being said. She tried to block them out, attempting, instead, to make sense of what had happened. To unravel her feelings. But that thread seemed to be well and truly tangled.

So she waited. A glance at the polished antique clock on the desk revealed that she had been waiting ten minutes. Which turned into an hour. Which turned into two. Every so often she would hear hurried steps and hushed, frantic voices. Whatever was going on out there it was certainly chaotic.

Helia's patience was growing thin. She knew she couldn't defy an order from Andreas, but waiting alone had her shoulders growing stiffer by the moment. Surely if they were going to tell her that it had all been mistake they would not have been gone this long—which made excitement once again flare in her belly. She tamped down hard on it.

Just when she had decided that it wouldn't matter if she waited here or in the library, where she could be alone, and where she would have a distraction, the door opened and in walked an irate Andreas. Carissa followed closely with a scowl, closing the door. He rounded the table to his throne-like seat, while she elegantly perched on the chair beside Helia's.

Andreas was a starchy character, but it had never concerned Helia before. Yet now she was filled with a sense of foreboding that warred with her earlier excitement and state of shock.

'I'm sure you have gathered as much, but I should officially tell you that King Leander is dead.'

That was obvious, but Helia would not interrupt until she could fully understand the situation she found herself in.

'Which means that Prince Vasili is now His Majesty,

the King of Thalonia. As such, he is required by law to marry and bear heirs.'

Heirs!

Silence pierced the air.

The hope, confusion, excitement all died. Helia could no longer feel that frantic heartbeat. Her jaw dropped as she pieced together what he meant. 'You're not serious!'

'I'm afraid I am.'

'Andreas, you cannot expect me to marry someone I don't even know.'

Marry and have children with them? That was completely unreasonable! She hadn't even thought about having family yet.

'This makes no sense. His Majesty cannot possibly want to marry someone he has never seen before,' she said, attempting to reason with them.

Yes, Helia had admired Prince Vasili for years. She had allowed herself fantasies of what it might be like if he one day took notice of her and it had felt good. Incredible. But never had those fantasies been like this.

'You can't take my choice away from me!'

'Look,' Andreas said in a severe tone, his fingers steepled under his chin, 'we are even less happy about this than you are, but whether we like it or not, Prince Vasili is now King and he has spoken. We have no choice but to obey.'

Irritation flashed through Helia. But Carissa nodded along with Andreas, as if agreeing to this absurdity.

'Whether you like it or not?' Helia asked. 'Is that because you disapprove of me, a commoner?' She directed this at Andreas—the person she had to report to in her responsibility over the palace archives, who didn't even have the good grace to look embarrassed. 'Or is it that you have a problem with King Vasili himself?'

'How long before we can get her and the country ready for the wedding?' Andreas asked Carissa, completely ignoring Helia's questions.

She felt a sharp pang of sympathy for Vasili. It was no secret what nobles thought of people like her, but to hold Vasili in such disregard was disrespectful, and she could only imagine hurtful to him. She remembered his reaction in the library, thinking that she would have been far less pleasant if the roles had been reversed. But his words had been reckless, and had very real consequences for her now.

She couldn't help the ember of anger burning in her from that. However, it was the two people with her in this room now who truly irked her. Their blatant disrespect for her and the King was entirely unacceptable. The way they looked at her, as if she was some kind of irritation they had to deal with, had her grinding her teeth. She wasn't the one who had put them in this situation. Vasili was. He was the one who had said the words, but even he wasn't entirely to blame.

'Don't ignore me,' she said.

Andreas cut a glare her way which she chose to disregard.

'No one has agreed to a wedding. What would this mean for me? My career?'

It was all too much. She needed them to spell out exactly what would happen to her—because right now she was completely overwhelmed.

'You would be Queen, of course,' Carissa said impatiently.

'And you would not return to your job,' Andreas added.

Helia's fingers curled in her skirt. Their tight grip was the only thing stopping her from hyperventilating. Her career was everything to her. She was a librarian, not a queen! What did she know about ruling?

Her stomach roiled at the thought.

She had spent two years among the palace's books and archives. Had scraped and clawed her way from nothing to end up here in the palace library.

Following her father's sudden passing when she was just a teenager, she had moved in with her uncle, her father's brother and business partner. He was meant to be her guardian, to take care of her, but he had only done so when it served him. Helia's father had left her a substantial inheritance—a nest egg meant to provide security for her when he could not—but she had never seen a penny of it as her uncle had cunningly taken it from her. And once he'd been in possession of it he had promptly dropped her off at the local orphanage. At a time when she had needed her family the most, she had been abandoned. Left to fend for herself. To deal with her grief and her anger alone.

She had found solace in books. Not that the orphanage had had very many. But they had filled her with a quiet happiness.

It had been no surprise to anyone, least of all herself, that she had become quiet and withdrawn. She hadn't been able to find it in herself to be the happy, effervescent person she had been with her father. She had been lost to her misery.

Only a single solitary spark had brightened those long, dark days.

While at school she had spent every free moment in the library. Until the librarian had taken pity on her and had allowed her to assist during breaks and after school. Bit by bit, in those dusty stacks, she had slowly come back to life. It was then that she had decided what she wanted to do with her life. She wanted to spend it among the books that had become her family and her escape. And she didn't want to be just a librarian at an underfunded, somewhat forgotten school. Oh, no, she wanted much more than that.

So she had earned herself a scholarship, and studied at one of the best universities in Thalonia, and immediately after that had gone to work at the city library in Seidon. Every day she would glimpse the palace on her commute to work and think to herself that one day she would work there. When the job she had dreamed of had finally become available, Helia had pounced on the opportunity. Now, at only twenty-eight, she was head librarian at the grandest library in the Kingdom, home to Thalonia's archives. It was a job she was immensely proud of.

They had another think coming if they thought she would take any of this lying down.

'What if I don't agree to this marriage?' she asked, interrupting their conversation.

Andreas dropped his hands to the carved armrests of his chair, staring Helia down. 'I don't want you to, Ms Demetriou. You are not the right queen for this kingdom. It goes against our traditions, not to mention brings us the nightmare challenge of getting you anywhere near ready to be a royal. But unfortunately for all of us King Vasili has decided, and none of us has the power to overturn his decision.'

His words were like a red rag to Helia, but she knew he was right. She wasn't ready to be Queen, and that would be a challenge, and Vasili had in fact picked her. His gaze had been intense. Filled with intent, but also grief and anger.

'I still haven't agreed.'

'Why wouldn't you agree?' Carissa very nearly sneered. 'Women don't often get the chance to become Queen.'

She's right, Helia thought to herself.

Most women never became Queen or gained any kind of power or influence, but the position had been presented to her now. It might not have occurred in a way she would have chosen, but surely there was an opportunity for her to make a difference.

Helia thought of those years at the orphanage, when funds had been low but there had been mouths to feed and growing bodies to clothe. When the temperature had dropped but they'd only been able to make do with what they had. When the children would talk about their dreams knowing they probably would never achieve them—because who would pay for their tuition?

She had come from among the forgotten citizens of not just Seidon, but Thalonia at large. Those without a voice who often just fell through the cracks. She remembered wishing she had the power to change things. Hoping that one day she would find a way to help. She had been volunteering at the orphanage whenever she could for years. A lot of those kids felt like her own. They were the closest thing she had to family.

Now there was a chance for one of the forgotten to sit on the throne, so maybe fighting this would be a mistake. It would be foolish of her to squander this opportunity—even if saying yes did mean that she would have to deal with attitudes like those of Andreas and Carissa every day.

Helia was conflicted. She didn't want to lose her career. It was all she had. All she loved. But she cared about the kind of children she'd grown up around…and beyond that there was Vasili.

She still remembered the day she had arrived at the palace. He had been the first royal she had seen. His beauty had rendered her speechless. With his short dark brown hair in soft, wavy curls and his golden-brown eyes, he had been a sight to behold. Let alone the fact that he had been climbing onto a black motorcycle at the time, clad in leathers.

He was the most unusual royal, and over the years she had noticed him more and more. Each time she did, a small attraction for the Prince grew. While she had almost never had any reason to directly interact with the royals, she'd noted how different he was compared to them. He always had a bit of time to chat to staff who were mostly treated as if they were invisible. He had a smile for everyone except when no one was watching him. But she did.

Helia was not delusional. She was entirely ordinary, and he had never once noticed her. Why would he? She spent all her time in the library that he never visited.

Now she felt foolish for feeling hopeful about being tied to him.

Her heart had skipped a beat when he had walked into the library today, in suit trousers and a button-down shirt that was open at the neck, but her appreciation had been halted by the expression on his face. He'd seemed to be caught somewhere between weariness and anguish…

Still, appreciating the Prince—or rather the King—didn't mean she could be a queen.

The mere thought had her hands trembling, and instilled a very real fear in her. She was confident around books, but had no idea how to navigate a royal court. She came from nothing. But didn't that make her perfect in a way? Vasili had been born to this life. He knew precisely what he was supposed to do. Could she show him what he *should* care about?

They were opposite forces, but together they could be something special. The thought filled her with equal parts trepidation and excitement.

'I'll do it.'

The moment the words left her lips, Helia's heart began to race.

'Of course you will.'

There was a look of smug satisfaction on Carissa's face that had annoyance bursting through Helia, eclipsing her nervousness.

'Think what you will, Carissa, but unless either of you can get His Majesty to change his mind I'm all you have—and I have my reasons for agreeing.'

Like the fact that *all* of Thalonia's people would be able to count on her, not just the rich and aristocratic, whether they realised it or not. Her every decision would have serious repercussions.

Her pulse hammered and her palms sweated. She tried to focus on her breathing. Panicking wouldn't help her.

She was still torn. Her whole life had been changed in a matter of minutes. The career she had fought for would be taken from her and replaced with something far more influential and terrifying. She hadn't really been given much choice, but her traitorous heart still beat just a little faster at the thought of being with Vasili.

Vasili sat in a plush white chair in Leander's office. *His* office. He had hardly ever come in here…the seat of power for Thalonia. He had hated this room with a passion growing up, and had been pleased when Leander had made changes to it. The walls still had frescoes from centuries long past. The blue of the sea was evident on nearly every wall, and the gold accents still glowed as if the metal had been poured straight onto the plaster, but everything else had changed.

Light poured in through the large arched windows, illuminating the white couches and the armchair where he sat. Towards the far end was a meeting table with six chairs, and directly in front of the window, as if all of Thalonia and the sea stood behind the man who sat there, was a behemoth of a desk.

An empty desk.

This office reflected Leander perfectly. How he'd tried to marry his modern views with a traditional past. It wasn't Vasili.

He leaned his head against a backrest carved in the Rococo style and closed his eyes, uttering a soft curse. He should never have lost his temper. It never helped any situation. But when he thought about Andreas and Carissa trying to foist a bride on him his blood started to boil all over again.

They were loyal to the crown, to Leander. The latter he could forgive, even respect, but the former...? That angered him immensely. Because wasn't that exactly like his parents? Loyal to the crown to the detriment of him?

Vasili understood that they were unhappy he would have to take over. But he didn't *have* to do anything. Not only had he never been meant to be King, but he also never wanted it—and he could only imagine who his 'trusted' advisors would pick for him to marry. Another thing he was simply expected to accept without consideration for how he felt. And for what? To save the crown? Why would he care? He hated it.

That was certainly no secret. All his life he'd wanted out, yet he knew he was stuck in his gilded cage—which was why he'd rebelled just now. As he always did. Except this rebellion made him feel guilty, because he had left no room for argument. He could only imagine how pushy that would have made Andreas and Carissa. The chaos his staff would now be consumed by as they navigated his decision.

A groan sounded through the silent office as he replayed

the moment he had chosen the librarian to be his wife. He didn't even know her name, for pity's sake! But even in that moment of madness he hadn't been able to help but notice how stunningly beautiful she was. Entirely arresting. Her eyes had brought to mind the untameable seas around the Kingdom.

He'd made a reckless decision, thinking Andreas would see it for what it was. See that he needed to grieve. He had just lost his brother. That still didn't feel entirely real. He needed time to come to terms with that…with these massive changes. But they hadn't seen that, or had simply ignored it, and Vasili knew time was something he was never going to get.

He had awoken that morning with two women in his bed and the thought that today would be like any other day. He had decided to ride down the coast, where a lavish party was planned for the evening.

A part of him still wanted to do that. To turn his back on the palace and forget all of it for a few hours.

He heaved a sigh and walked to the large window, staring out at Seidon. Earlier he had had the thought that he would like to let the crown fall into ruin. He really liked that idea. More than ever the temptation to abdicate seduced him. He wanted to reach out and grab on to that notion with both hands. Leave it all and walk away. He liked his life as it was.

Vasili had just decided a ride on his motorcycle was precisely what he needed when he heard the door open. He knew who it was before he even spoke.

'Here you are, Your Majesty,' said Andreas, as he entered and quietly shut the door behind him.

Vasili was struck with a vivid fantasy of throwing the man out. He had seen far too much of him for one day. He

wanted to ask if Andreas was done with terrorising the librarian, but he said nothing. While he might not have received quite the same training as Leander, Vasili knew how
to use silence as a show of power, and something told him
he would always have to wield that power with Andreas.

Turning around with his hands clasped behind his back,
he pinned Andreas with a stare that had the older man stopping before he could cross the room all the way.

Andreas cleared his throat. 'We have spoken to Helia
Demetriou, sir, but we need to discuss this decision. She
isn't what this kingdom needs.'

'I suppose you know exactly what that is?' Vasili challenged.

'In this instance, yes. We need a queen who can take the
throne immediately. She cannot do that. We have no time.
King Leander's wedding has been planned. Every vendor is
confirmed. Every part of his wedding was meant to show-
case Thalonia to the world, and people are still relying on
us to move forward with the event. As much as it might
hurt us, we need you and a queen on the throne. We need
the coronation to happen as soon as possible, or we risk
damaging our people financially. That takes priority. God
forbid, but should something happen to you, Thalonia will
be in serious trouble. We need to have faith that the Queen
could rule in that situation.'

A spare ruler. Not just that, now he was to be a filler-in
at someone else's wedding. His life truly meant nothing.
Vasili was a spare in every way.

All he could do was shake his head.

'Allow me to speak freely,' Andreas went on.

'Nothing has stopped you before.'

'The wedding has to go ahead. But Carissa and I feel
that while Miss Demetriou has agreed, we believe we

could come up with a better solution. I'm sure she has her appeal…she just isn't the best choice given our time constraints. We will have the entire staff running around trying to arrange a wedding, a coronation and training—which ordinarily would be far simpler than what we have to do now. Which is to teach someone how to be royal. I have got people trying to figure out how to impart an entire lifetime's worth of training and knowledge in a few short weeks. But this isn't going to work. It's an impossible task.'

Vasili still said nothing. He simply cocked a brow, indicating for him to continue.

'Please, Your Majesty, just listen.'

Vasili didn't want to. He knew he was being ridiculous—but so was this entire situation.

'So what would you propose? Hmm? A marriage to someone I would have nothing to do with?'

'It doesn't have to be that way. Princess Allegra is still an option—'

'You have to be out of your mind! I am not marrying Leander's fiancée.'

The idea was abhorrent.

'She understands how to rule. She is ready to be Queen and you have tolerated her in the past.'

'Tolerated? Is that how low the bar is for a royal consort?'

The bite in Vasili's words had Andreas flinching.

'She is one option, and there are other options that you need to look at for the good of the Kingdom. We would have to alter our traditions, our processes, to accommodate Helia. How long would that take? You know Princess Allegra—you know nothing about the librarian.'

That was true. He knew nothing about her. But he would take her over any of the royals he knew. Any of the nobility. And if it took time to ready her to be queen then that was all the better for him. At least he would get the time he needed then.

'Your parents knew each other as children. They were both of noble blood and were probably the most loved royals we have ever had on the throne.'

Except they hadn't loved each other. They hadn't loved him.

'I have said it before and I will say it again, Andreas. I am neither my parents nor Leander. You'd best stop expecting to see them in me. I don't care what you have to do—that isn't my problem. No matter how many times you come to me with this, my decision will not change.'

'Vasili!' Andreas snapped. His frustration was pouring off him in waves.

'Excuse me?' Vasili all but growled.

Andreas took a very deep breath. 'Apologies, Your Majesty, but you don't seem to be listening. We *cannot* make this happen. Not in the time we have.'

'Andreas,' Vasili said, with a calm he did not feel, especially when the fuse of his temper had once again been lit. 'I've had just about as much disrespect as I am going to take from you, and this will be the last time. I understand your panic, but my word is final. Now, bring Miss Demetriou to me. I wish to speak to her in private.'

There was no emotion in Vasili's voice. Every swirling thought and feeling was locked away securely deep within him.

'Of course.'

He watched Andreas leave and turned back to the window. He needed to find out why Helia had agreed and then give her an opportunity to back out. After all, this wasn't a decision he had made for her—it was a decision he had made against being the King they wanted.

It wasn't long before Vasili heard footsteps on the other side of the door. Silently it swung open and in she walked. She took the breath from him. He couldn't speak. All he could do was stare. How had he never noticed her before? She had to be the most exquisite creature ever to have graced the palace.

It took a gargantuan effort to wrestle his thoughts back into something that made sense. He had called her here for a reason.

Clearing his throat, Vasili instructed her to close the door and take a seat.

Of all the things she could have done, she curtseyed.

'Your Majesty,' she said politely, and did as she was told.

The action was so at odds with how his day had gone, Vasili did well to hide his laughter.

He followed her with his eyes as she sat down. 'Given our current situation, I think we are past formalities, wouldn't you say? Call me Vasili.'

'My name is Helia,' she replied in a soft voice.

For the first time since he'd been told his brother had died, Vasili wanted to genuinely smile. She was a little gauche, and he couldn't help but find it endearing. She was a lamb in a den of wolves. A woman like her should never be shackled to a debaucher. Especially not one who held the throne in such contempt.

'I would ask you how you are, but I imagine you have no good answer right now, and for that I must apologise.'

'I appreciate that, Your— Vasili.'

Her skin was tinged red and Vasili had the mad impulse to run his fingers over it. Would she feel hot to the touch?

He took a steadying breath. Seeing Helia in front of him

had brought home just what he had set in motion. 'I realise I have placed us in a difficult situation, but I want you to know that you can be honest with me. In fact, I insist on it. And I will do the same. Understood?'

Helia nodded.

'I need you to say the words, Helia.'

He saw the flash of her pupils dilating and he imagined a different circumstance when he might say those same words. Her name felt like a caress on his tongue.

'I understand.'

'Why are you agreeing to this madness? Surely you were given the choice to refuse me?'

Helia looked away. Wavy caramel curls fell over curved shoulders, and she avoided his gaze before she straightened, and looked him in the eye. At first Vasili had thought her meek. Timid. Now he could see there was fire in her. It shouldn't tempt him as much as it did.

'If I can make a difference to people as Queen, in any way, I would be a fool to say no. I may be a commoner, but I think that gives me a voice few ever get to use. I know better than most what it's like to be forgotten.'

Vasili walked to the front of the large desk and perched on the edge, getting as close to Helia as he dared without touching her. 'What do you mean?'

But she didn't respond. He couldn't blame her. He had asked for honesty, but not for her to bare her secrets. Even if she seemed attracted to him, she didn't know him, and she had no reason to answer. So he respected her silent request for him not to push.

'Helia, you are not being forced to accept this situation. If you feel there are needs not being met in our kingdom… if you feel that you need to be the voice of those without one…that's fine. You can talk to me and I will listen. You don't have to sacrifice your life for it. Regardless of what anyone says, you have a choice. You always have a choice.'

He hadn't anticipated that things would reach this point, but he now realised that he had doubled down on his decision only because Andreas had caused him to snap. He'd reacted in the way he always did. By resisting.

Helia was trying desperately to banish the flight of butterflies in her stomach. Her heart was racing, as it had been since she'd walked into the office. Having worked at the palace for two years, she knew exactly how to behave in the presence of royalty, and she was certain she had always come across as polite and self-contained. Yet from the moment she'd walked into this room she had been overwhelmed by the new King's presence.

It took a mammoth effort for her to focus on the words he had been saying. It seemed surreal that he was saying them, and speaking had become difficult.

'I respect that,' Helia said, trying to keep the wobble of nerves from her voice.

He had told her to be honest, but she didn't know if her thoughts were too bold to say out loud.

'Whatever is on your mind, you can say it, Helia.'

She wasn't so sure about that…

'You have agreed to be Queen,' Vasili said with a small smirk. 'How are you going to do that if you can't talk to me?'

She had agreed, and now she wondered if that had been a terrible mistake. What was she thinking? She couldn't be the King's equal. But she couldn't waste a chance to help the orphanage.

'I will offer you a thought if you offer me one. Does that sound fair?' he asked.

She nodded, still unsure and feeling completely out of her depth.

'I'm wondering how you could agree to this. If you're actually okay with the thought of being Queen…of being married to me. I see how tense you are and I think that you aren't okay, and that this world I live in might be more cut-throat than you are prepared to handle.'

Helia hadn't realised how perceptive he was. Of course she hadn't. She had never been in his company long enough to notice anything. She hated it that he was probably right. She didn't know how to deal with royal business, and that in particular scared her. As honourable as her intentions were, the worry that she might fail spectacularly as Queen still sat at the back of her mind.

Helia swallowed thickly. Vasili had spoken his thoughts—his doubts—and in doing so had shown her it was safe for her to express hers, even if it made her un-comfortable.

'It seems to me that you do not wish to marry.' Whether it was to marry her or marry in general, she didn't know. She couldn't blame him for not wanting her, she was en-tirely ordinary compared to him—the antithesis to the women he was normally seen with. 'Surely you could choose not to. You are King and you are entitled to grieve.'

Vasili shook his head, a sombre look passing over his features. 'If only that were true. It's best you find out now that being a royal doesn't leave you with much room for choice. This…' he waved his hand between them '…will be the last big decision you get to make on your own. Ev-erything you do from now on, everything you say, will be watched and dissected. Andreas and Carissa are only the start of it. I made a reckless pronouncement that affects you…how much time did you get before you were forced to make a decision? How much choice were you given?'

He was right. She hadn't been given much choice or any time to digest what had happened. And once she'd agreed she had been almost immediately brought to the King. She was in a tailspin, fighting to gain control. But she had had no choices most of her life. She'd had to survive. And even though she was finally comfortable and thriving, she knew she could survive again.

'Even as a commoner you don't get many choices. You have to make do with what you're dealt.' She hoped she'd hidden the deep sorrow that lanced through her.

'Don't call yourself that. Andreas may have certain ideas about tradition and propriety, but I do not share them. There is nothing common about you.'

The vehemence in his words had Helia's heart skipping a beat. He made her feel off balance, and she desperately wanted to believe that he thought her something special. It was beginning to dawn on her just how out of her depth she truly was. Wishing to share a moment with Vasili should have been the last thing on her mind—she should be singularly focussed on what it meant to be Queen. Who she was doing this for.

All that thought did was make her panic.

'If you agree to this, Helia, it will not be an easy life.'

'Life isn't easy anyway.'

She bit her lip to stop herself saying more and his gaze flashed to her mouth, darkening. The atmosphere between them seemed to change. Become charged with something intoxicating. Her eyes darted to his lips, but quickly flicked up, meeting his. Heat flared within her.

'No, it isn't.' Vasili's voice came low and raspy. 'I didn't intend for you to get caught up in this battle. The decision I made was meant to do nothing more than—'

'Shock?' she offered, forgetting herself, lost in his golden-brown gaze.

Vasili's lips twitched with a suppressed smile. 'Yes. And just meant to earn me a reprieve.'

'The next few weeks are going to be difficult,' he warned, curling his fingers around the edge of the table to stop himself from reaching out to Helia.

'I expect so. But I'm not backing out of this.'

It was barely above a whisper.

'Why?'

She looked away, her fingers fidgeting, and for a moment he thought she wouldn't answer.

'A lot of people helped me. As Queen, I can be there for them and so many more. No one else cares about them, but I do.'

'You will lose any semblance of a life. Your career. Is that what you want?'

She continued to stare down at her hands. He wanted to force her to look at him.

When she answered, her voice was strong. 'No, it's not. But we can only work with the cards we are dealt. May I ask you a question?'

'Of course.'

'You don't want to get married...'

'No, I don't. I probably never will want that.'

'Then what *do* you want?'

It was the question Vasili had wanted to hear all his life. It was sad that the only person to ask was someone with no power to change anything. Still, he'd promised her honesty, so he would answer.

'To leave. The throne…this kingdom. All of it.'

'Then why don't you?'

'Because, as much as I would love to abdicate, the well-being of the people rests on my shoulders. I would love nothing more than to cast it all away, but unfortunately I was born to a duty that I can't escape.'

Vasili hated the defeat in his voice. Earlier he had wanted to climb on his bike and leave, but no matter where he went he knew the truth of the matter wouldn't change. He had to be King.

'So where does that leave us?' Helia asked softly.

It left him with little choice. It left him with a kingdom to run and a marriage he didn't want. His sole choice was either to marry the beautiful woman before him, or a royal that his staff approved of.

He realised he had taken too long to answer when Helia stood and with a glance back at him walked to the door.

Except he couldn't let her walk out yet.

His steps ate up the distance between them, and just as she placed her hand on the door he flattened his palm against the wood, preventing her from opening it. Standing behind her, he could finally truly see what a delicate thing she was. Her head would comfortably tuck under his chin. But he left the smallest of spaces between their bodies.

He bent down slightly, his lips close to her ear. 'Be sure you want to go through with this, Helia. The crown…this world… It is not made up of good people. It's full of people like me.'

She turned around then, leaning back against the door. Her tempting body was almost underneath him. That fire was back in her eyes. Raging in full force and calling to him.

'You are King now. The crown can be whatever you want it to be.'

Who *was* this bewitching creature?

Vasili ached to know more about her. He was filled with a curiosity he had never experienced before. He wanted to touch her. To run the backs of his fingers down her cheek. To brush his lips against hers. They were nothing to each other, but she had woven some sort of spell around him, because for the first time that day he could breathe. Helia had pushed away the forces suffocating him.

And so he had his answer. He would marry Helia over anyone Andreas chose. At least she would be his choice. But, given that he didn't wish to marry at all, he still didn't feel like it—which made him want to lash out. Except he couldn't. So he simply withdrew into himself and stepped away from Helia, feeling the fight in him go out.

'To answer your question, it leaves neither of us much of a choice.'

'So we'll marry,' Helia said.

It wasn't a question. Merely an agreement.

'Yes. Your life as you knew it is over. I'm sorry.'

CHAPTER THREE

HELIA STOOD IN the antechamber of her suite, which functioned as a receiving room. The luxury she found herself in was not something she could get used to. She had been given these splendid rooms the day she'd agreed to be Queen, and she had been in shock then. She wasn't entirely sure that it had worn off yet.

There were paintings on her ceiling! And Helia was certain her whole apartment would have fit numerous times into this suite.

She hadn't been allowed to return home. Her belongings has been sent for. As Vasili had warned her, once she'd agreed, she'd had little choice.

Two weeks. That was how long it had been since Helia had given the King her word that she would marry him. And that time had been filled with what she called her 'Queen Lessons'.

Being a librarian had given her vast knowledge on many different topics. She was proud of how well read she was. But no level of intelligence or knowledge could have prepared her for this.

Every single day was filled with lessons on politics, decorum, history… She'd had every part of her scrutinised. From her posture to her table manners to her appearance.

It made her feel lacking in a way she had never considered before. She'd been given a list of literature that it would be appropriate for a queen to have read. She didn't mind that so much—at least she had the books for company—but she loathed being told what she was 'permitted' to read. She'd let it go for now, keeping her eyes on the reason she was doing any of this. Besides, when she was Queen her requests would not be ignored. Or so she hoped.

She had even been made to undergo a physical examination with the private royal physician, and it seemed so had Vasili—as evidenced by the copy of his all-clear results that was given to her. It made sense, considering they expected her to bear his children at some point. But she still didn't know how she felt about that.

She required a great deal of patience, as every 'lesson' was filled with jabs at her background. Comments on how the lessons would not be necessary if she were a royal. Whispers that she should not be going on the throne. That her very presence had thrown their plans into disarray. Helia was set to be their queen, and yet none of them saw fit to hide their disdain.

All it did was make her square her shoulders and lift her chin. She would show them that she would not let them drag her down, even if their words pierced her armour and broke down what little confidence she had.

Those two frantic weeks had gone by in the blink of an eye. And now here she was. Standing alone in her suite in the most spectacular wedding dress she had ever seen. A sheath of fine, hand-made lace, it caressed her chest and fell to the floor. She touched the band of lace around her upper arms, exposing her golden shoulders. The full-length mirror that had been placed in the room reflected a woman who looked like her, but couldn't possibly be.

She turned slightly, admiring the way the dress hugged every part of her. From below her shoulder blades all the way down, ending in a long, dramatic train. It reminded her of the bubbly wash along the shore as the waves broke.

Perhaps it had reminded others of it too. Which would explain the sapphire and diamond tiara in her hair, which had been styled into an elegant chignon. It sparkled like a sprinkling of the sea. There were sapphires in her ears too. Dainty little drops that would take no attention away from the masterpiece that was the dress.

My wedding dress, she thought, her hands growing clammy.

She tried taking deep calming breaths as the full extent of what she was about to embark upon crashed over her. Was she doing the right thing? What if all the whispers were true? She was an orphan who had come from nothing. Would she be an adequate queen? Did she have any right to believe she could be?

Helia turned to fully face her reflection in the mirror, wondering if she had been naïve about the reality of her future. But these doubts were her own to bear. She couldn't back out now. This was her only way to help all the forgotten people, like herself when she was in the care system. Most kids from the orphanage didn't grow into powerful adults. They became people just doing what they could to get by. She was one of the lucky ones, and fortune had truly smiled down on her. It would be foolish to think there wouldn't be a price to pay for it. So she would use whatever royal power she could to help those who meant the most to her.

She was under no illusions. Helia knew this would be one of the hardest challenges she would ever have to navigate. But she stood on the precipice of fulfilling a wish she had held so dear for all these years. A wish that she could make a difference.

And there was another reason why she couldn't back out. One that felt as vital as breathing. She'd given Vasili her word. He'd given her a chance to back out and she had said she wouldn't. That promise might mean little to him, but it meant something important to her—because she had made it to *him*.

She was well aware that he didn't want this marriage, but duty had given him no choice. She had to find a way to get him on her side and keep him there, so that she could realise her plans. She would have to learn to be the Queen he needed. Yet another thing to make her feel uneasy...

Helia hadn't seen Vasili at all in the two weeks that had passed. The lessons had taken up all of her time, and she assumed he had been coming to terms with being king. So there had been silence. She supposed she could have reached out in some way—but so could he. At the end of each day she'd been so tired she'd often fallen asleep as soon as she'd collapsed on her bed. She hadn't even been allowed back to the library, which had made her miserable. But at least she had the comfort of some books in her room.

She didn't know what to expect when she walked down the aisle. There had been no dress rehearsals. Andreas and Carissa had simply explained the order of events to her.

Would Vasili be there at the end of the aisle? Or would he choose to go against the wishes of his advisors? What would she do if he wasn't there? He had admitted that he wanted to leave. She remembered with great clarity the remoteness in him when they had agreed to marry. His reluctance.

It had stung, but she couldn't hold it against him.

She took a deep breath. Then another. Falling down this

spiral would help nothing. She had a duty. If Vasili wasn't at the altar, she would deal with it then.

A firm knock sounded on the door and she whirled around just as Andreas walked into the room, dressed in a tailcoat.

'Good, you're ready.'

Helia was used to his lack of greeting by now, as if he was far too busy to waste even precious seconds.

'I think you could pass for a queen already.'

'I think that could almost pass for a compliment,' she retorted.

Her relationship with Andreas was now in a rather odd place. He was no longer her boss. In fact, once she was Queen she would be much higher up the hierarchy than him. But he still had far more knowledge of this royal world than she did. His disdain for her was certainly still on display, but it couldn't last for ever. She would learn what she had to in order to deal with all the palace staff—including him.

'Perhaps.' He stepped fully into the room and closed the door behind him. 'How are you feeling?'

'A little ill,' she said truthfully.

'To be expected. Just remember what you're supposed to do and say, and it will be fine.'

Helia nodded. As pre-wedding pep talks went, Andreas's attempt was abominable, but she hadn't really expected comfort from him.

'The carriage is outside,' he informed her, before taking a step closer. 'And my offer to walk you down the aisle still stands.'

'I appreciate that, but my answer is still no, thank you.'

'That isn't our tradition.'

Helia wanted to say that neither was the King marrying someone who wasn't of noble birth, but she held her tongue.

Andreas had made the offer several times. She knew it wasn't out of kindness but rather wanting the right image. But she had always known that she would have no one to walk her down the aisle if she ever married. Her father had died, and no one else deserved the honour.

Helia had had to rely on herself for a long time, and she wasn't the only one who did so. The world she came from was filled with people just like her, so she would walk herself. It would be a show of strength and solidarity for them, even though it was another break in tradition.

'Shall we?' She gestured to the door.

Andreas held it open and several women stepped into the room, each of them holding up part of the long, lacy train of her dress as they set off through the palace and then helped her into a waiting carriage, pulled by four magnificent white horses. The carriage itself was white, with gilding and hints of lapis lazuli. Pure opulence.

As soon as the door was closed, they set off for the cathedral.

Vasili stood at the altar of the largest cathedral in Seidon. Alone. There were cameras all over the place. As discreet as they tried to be, he still saw them. Media trucks crowded much of the square outside. The royal wedding was being televised throughout the nation. Vasili pretended they didn't exist. This wedding was a show. He found nothing sacred in it.

He cast his gaze down the long aisle, where a thick red carpet had been laid over the stone floors. Pillars topped with elaborate white flower arrangements stood proud on either side. Light filtering in from the high windows illuminated them. Slight shadows played on the sculptures attached to the columns that towered all the way up to the vaulted ceiling. Row upon row of people dripping in wealth sat in their finery, waiting for the arrival of the would-be queen.

Vasili ignored all of them. He kept his eyes firmly fixed on the closed doors, standing almost preternaturally still with his hands clasped at his back. His only movement was running his thumb back and forth along the gold accents on the cuff of his jacket. He was decked in full royal regalia. A gold sash sat over his jacket and there was a ceremonial sword at his waist. He felt ridiculous in the uniform. He would never have worn it given the choice, but nothing about what was happening was about choice. He knew he projected the kind of image a king should. Strong and regal. Inside, he wanted that door to open so they could get this wedding over with.

Standing alone meant he had every eye on him. Having someone beside him would have diluted the attention, but he hadn't wanted anyone to stand with him. The only person who should have had the privilege was dead. And, while he was getting married and ensuring Thalonia's future, he wanted no one to forget that Leander was gone. One king was dead and he had already been replaced by another. There was a celebration planned, and a coronation would follow the wedding. He found it all repugnant.

This should have been Leander's wedding, not his. Vasili would have happily stood beside his brother. He was the one groomed for the life of a king. He could almost hear fate's shrill laugh as he waited for his bride to arrive so he could become the King no one had asked for. But, no matter how much he hated the situation he was in, this was the very reason for which he had been born. A fact he'd had to come to terms with over the last few weeks. He hadn't seen Helia at all during that time, but she hadn't been far from his mind.

The image of her pinned beneath him against the door assaulted him frequently. Particularly in his dreams, when he would wake up hard and panting. It was perhaps a mistake to have kept his distance. Andreas had informed him of her progress during her lessons. The older man's disapproval had leaked into every report, but it had made him smile. Vasili cursed himself now, because he could have used that time to get to know her. See if they had anything in common. Find out what she loved other than books—because he was yet to meet a librarian who didn't. Truly get to the bottom of why she was martyring herself like this.

Perhaps rebellion was so rooted in him that he had hated what was occurring so much that avoiding Helia had been just another way to rebel against the crown. It was a belated realisation, he knew, because now they were on the verge of getting married and he still wished to bolt from the church.

The doors slowly swung open, and it was officially too late.

How did she feel about him staying away? he wondered. The palace was already full of pretentious snobs—he could only imagine how lonely the past two weeks must have been for her. He regretted his actions now. He should have given her a way to contact him. After all, it was his fault that she was being taken from her comfortable life.

Was she reluctant to go through with this wedding? Was she nervous? Would she walk through those doors at all? Given how he felt towards the throne, he wouldn't hold it against her if she decided not to show up. He had certainly given her reason not to say yes. No doubt Andreas would quickly take the opportunity to find him a different bride. One who fitted in with his idea of the perfect queen.

He half expected to see the man walk in now, to tell him his bride had left. And for some reason the idea of not seeing those caramel curls or those blue eyes felt like a loss he didn't want to endure. But then the hum of numerous people getting to their feet sounded through the cathedral and a lone violin played chords that were both beautiful and sorrowful, making the hairs on Vasili's arms rise.

But it wasn't the music that stole his breath. It wasn't the magnificent building with all its rich history. The sole reason he felt as if he was in the crushing depths of the sea, with no air in his lungs, was the woman standing in the doorway. Her curled hair was pulled back, with a few loose tendrils framing her face, catching the filtered light like a corona around her...a divine crown. He didn't blame anyone for the gasps he heard echo around the chamber. If he'd had any air he might have gasped too.

She stood alone, just like him. A pillar of regal strength. And he felt it then: her eyes latching on to his as she glided down the aisle. Her dress trailed long after her in an ocean of lace, as if she carried the sea wherever she went. A more perfect queen he could not imagine. Vasili hadn't even known of Helia until just two weeks ago, and now he wondered how a secret like her could ever have been kept in this place.

She was utterly, heartbreakingly beautiful.

He didn't expect the swift punch of guilt that came next. This stunning woman was an innocent. He knew nothing about her. Perhaps she had a life she loved. Maybe she loved being in that library. And just because she'd happened to be in the wrong place at the wrong time, he had dragged her into this madness with him. Vasili had thought of her as a secret, and maybe she'd been safer that way. Because the moment he had seen her, he had turned her world upside down. For that there should be no forgiveness. He deserved his punishment of life as the King he didn't want to be, locked in a loveless marriage he didn't want, but there was no way Helia deserved that fate. She deserved a life of pure happiness. Especially since back in his office he'd sensed a hardship she didn't want to talk about.

But he couldn't stop the wedding. Not now. It would cause unspeakable embarrassment to her, and he just didn't have it in him to be that cruel.

As Helia drew close, the corner of her mouth kicked up just the tiniest fraction, and he returned her small smile with one of his own. He held out his hand once she was close enough, feeling a current tingle across his palms as her skin made contact with his. He helped her up the small step.

'Hello, Vasili,' she whispered as she came to stand in front of him.

He swore he could see relief on her face. Had she been worried that he wouldn't be here? He supposed he'd given her no reason to trust that he would.

'Helia.'

He smiled down at her, taking her in. From the tiara on her head to the lace band around her bare arms, to the dress that kissed the ground with her every movement.

Vasili lost the battle of trying not to touch her, grazing his finger along what was hardly a sleeve. He pulled his hand back as the bishop let out an amused chuckle. He barely heard the man speak. All he could concentrate on was Helia. So he took her hands in his, and immediately the calm he had felt in her presence before descended upon him.

It was more than calm. It was as if every ounce of his attention was being drawn to one place. Helia. To that hum between their bodies. To the current travelling along their skin. There was temptation here.

'Vasili…' Helia whispered with a tiny smile, urging him to pay attention.

He heard the bishop gently clear his throat.

He was so focused on Helia that he hadn't even noticed it that the moment in which he would have to promise himself to her was upon them. The moment when he would have to say words he didn't believe in. He still did not want to be married, but there was no way around this, so with great effort he held his frustration at bay and made his vows.

He slid a large blue gem onto her finger. The French cut blue diamond reflected the light infinitely, like crushed ice, as the two smaller white diamonds on either side twinkled prettily in their platinum setting. The jewel had been in his family for generations, but none of the previous Queens had worn it. All had opted for something far more garish, but he couldn't think of a better suited choice. Helia was different from all those who had come before her, and that was something worth celebrating.

'Vasili…' Helia's voice rang out sweet and clear. 'I take you to be my husband, for better, for worse, to love and to cherish. And to stand by you alone, for all of our days.'

He didn't understand the feeling that overcame him at hearing those added words.

Helia had fire in her and would not bend to the will of others. Not easily at least. Understanding her message, he couldn't help but smile. She would stand by him alone. Not by Andreas or Carissa or the demands of the crown. She had just announced to all of Thalonia that she intended to be his partner.

You are King now. The crown can be whatever you want it to be.

He would have her support to do just that.

'You may now kiss the bride.'

Vasili heard the words. The moment he had craved and dreaded was upon him. For two weeks he had wanted to kiss her. Images of her against the door of his office flashed in his mind once again. He had wanted a taste of her then, and after replaying that moment so frequently he wasn't sure that he would be able to stop once his lips met hers.

So, with her hands still in his, Vasili mustered every bit of control he had and leaned in, placing a chaste kiss upon her lips. But as if it were a trap, designed just for him, that one simple touch caused the very air to snap around them.

He couldn't stop kissing her if he tried.

A buzzing warmth trailed over him from the contact of their lips, winding through his body, until his arms went around her and her hands found their way to his chest.

He couldn't think. Couldn't breathe. This innocent kiss was more overwhelming than any he had had before. Every other kiss he'd experienced in his life had been a means to an end. Merely a seduction to make the pay-off greater. Every one of those fell into the shadow of this one.

Without even realising it, he brought up a hand to cup her face, angling his head to kiss her more deeply. And, as if they had danced this particular dance before, she moved with him, opening to him as his tongue caressed hers. Igniting his blood.

He swallowed the sigh she breathed into him.

He'd thought there was nothing sacred about this wedding, but he found the divine in Helia's pillowy lips. She was soft and sweet and tentative. Everything he realised he had been imagining she would be, but more. Calm and crazed. Trapped and free. This embrace devoured him. Her eager responses spurred him on to kiss her harder, deeper.

He was utterly lost to the current that swept them both away, and it was only the sound of polite clapping and an amused chuckle close by that broke through the haze, wrenching him back.

With careful tenderness he pulled away, noticing the look in Helia's eyes, like a raging sea. And he knew she was just as affected as he was.

Maybe there was an up-side to this marriage after all.

CHAPTER FOUR

THE CORONATION FOLLOWED immediately after the wedding ceremony.

Vasili knelt on the step in the cathedral with Helia by his side and Helia glanced sidelong at him. She could see how hard he was gritting his teeth. She herself trembled on the inside. This feeling was far beyond nervousness. This was fear. Anxiety that she couldn't control but couldn't show either. She just had to dig down deeper, to find a way to fake the calm serenity the world expected from her.

But the fear refused to abate. She was terrified she would fail. She knew she already had with her little act of defiance. Adding to her vows made her a failure as Queen because she hadn't done what was expected of her. But she and Vasili had agreed on honesty. Besides that, he was King. She needed to show she was on his side, and maybe then he would be on hers.

Once their coronation oaths were said and the ceremony was over, Vasili offered Helia his arm, which she took with a small smile, letting him lead them out of the cathedral and into the square where their carriage awaited.

Helia waved to the people, ensuring her smile never faltered. A mask that would hide her nerves and help her do exactly as she was told.

Helia couldn't forsake her defiant heart. After all, it was what had helped her survive her years in the orphanage and beyond. Adding to her marriage vows was proof of that, but she would still take instruction on how to provide the right image for Thalonia's queen. She had to appease Andreas to a certain degree—and more than that she had no idea how to be Queen. It was a tightrope to walk, but she had to do it for the orphanage.

For herself.

For Vasili.

She could feel his burning gaze on her skin, but she refused to look at him. She was afraid of what she would see. Afraid that she would expose her attraction to him. Afraid that her mind would morph whatever that look was on his face into some sort of lie, telling her he wanted her too.

She couldn't lose her head.

The palace drew closer, and when the gilded carriage finally stopped Vasili stepped out and then placed his hands on Helia's waist. Her eyes locked with his as he lifted her out. His hands tightened around her, the touch rendering her breathless. His hold had safe. Steady. As if he wouldn't let her falter.

Helia knew that was just the hope in her heart talking and she had to control it.

'One more show, Helia,' he said to her softly, setting her on her feet.

'I know. Are you ready?'

'No, but let's do it anyway.'

'I feel like that might be a theme for our reign,' she said.

She laughed, covering up the way her heart pounded from the thought of what they were about to do. From his proximity.

Vasili chuckled. A look of surprise flashed across his face. 'Come, Your Majesty, your adoring public awaits.'

She saw straight through Vasili's attempt at levity. There was an intensity about him that was entirely at odds with his words. He hated this, but he needed to play his part just as she was.

They walked through the palace in silence, making their way to the second floor, where they stopped before a set of closed double doors. He unlinked their arms as he turned to face her, placing his hands on her shoulders. It was as if he was bidding her to look only at him.

As if she could look anywhere else.

'Once we go out there, every person in the world will know who you are. Your privacy will be non-existent. Do you need a minute?'

She had been more apprehensive about this part than any of the others, because now she would be on show as Queen of the land. Every other part of the ceremony had been behind closed doors. It had felt controlled. But now she had to face the people and put on an act that Andreas would approve of. One that would reflect well on Vasili. All the while feeling like a fraud.

'I'm fine,' she said with a smile.

'And I'm going to remind you to be honest,' he said.

She glanced out through the doors, made up of numerous panes of glass, at the crowd beyond. 'I'm nervous—of course I am—but delaying helps no one.'

'If you're sure?'

'Do *you* need a minute?'

'More like several years. Let's get this over with.'

She nodded as he laced their fingers together, her heart jolting at the touch, and then, as one, they opened the doors and stepped out onto the balcony to face the crowd gathered just beyond the gates.

* * *

They might have clapped or cheered or waved flags. Vasili couldn't tell. All he felt was the weight of his new role. The consequences if he should fail. It wouldn't be he who suffered, but the ocean of people he now looked upon. Helia was waving. With the ever-present Andreas and Carissa at their backs, she didn't put a foot wrong—but he would not perform.

They were meant to share a kiss on this balcony. It was what every media outlet was waiting for. The perfect picture to splash on every news site and newspaper in Thalonia and beyond.

Vasili clamped his jaw shut. There was no way he would be kissing Helia in front of all these people. Not when the risk was getting sucked into that space where it was just him and her and this maddening attraction that he didn't want.

As soon as they were back inside and the doors had closed, Vasili handed his mantle to Andreas before helping Helia out of hers. Without another word to his private secretary, he escorted her to the King's quarters.

It was an enormous suite, with a luxurious sitting room. Beyond that was a pair of double doors, and the largest and grandest sleeping quarters in the palace. A second door off the sitting room led to the adjoining Queen's rooms, but Vasili wouldn't take Helia there.

'Make yourself comfortable. This is where you will sleep.'

'Where are you going?'

As much as he felt like a cad for doing so, Vasili didn't answer her. Her presence was a constant current, zapping over his skin. He could still feel her lips on his. And, heaven help him, he wanted to kiss her again. But there were too many warring emotions in him. Too many thoughts. He needed some space to re-centre.

'You can call for anything you need.'

He took her in one more time, standing there in her wedding dress with a look of confusion that quickly morphed into a blank slate.

'Vasili, we have a role to play here.'

He knew that.

'We have both made sacrifices today.'

Something else he was well aware of. But he couldn't be in this room with Helia a second longer without her affecting his judgement.

'You're right—we have. And it will make no difference to what happens tomorrow or the day after once I'm out through that door.'

'I can understand you needing to escape. I sympathise. But I have given up a great deal, and with Andreas watching my every step I can't afford to put a foot wrong. I've done everything expected of me today. I can support you, but I need you to do the same.'

Helia calling him out shouldn't have any effect on him, but damn him if her defiance didn't appeal to him. Still, he bowed to no one, and even though she had just become his queen and his wife, she would not be the exception.

'You *have* done well. But no one—not even you, Helia— gets to dictate to me.'

She nodded once and he left, making a bee line for his old bedroom.

The second the door snicked shut he ripped off his ceremonial baldric. It and his sword were tossed aside, before he dropped into the dark leather chair in the corner of the room.

As soon as he was old enough Vasili had removed every

hint of the palace from this space. His sanctuary. Now it was modern, with dark wooden floors and walls so blue it felt like being in the crushing depths of the sea. The artwork above his headboard certainly reminded him of water, and this was where he needed to be to centre himself.

Staring out of the window, he ran his finger along his lip and cursed. He was still thinking of that kiss. Of how much he'd wanted to kiss her in the carriage and again in the King's suite. But he knew it wouldn't have stopped there, so he'd had to escape.

Because that kiss had been different. It had made him feel instead of just being a physical indulgence. That kiss had made him need Helia, even though he never needed anyone. It had made him want to do anything, be anything, so he could keep kissing her. He had been so ready to give in to their chemistry after their kiss. Had thought that maybe they could have a little fun in this marriage… But it felt like a risk.

She already had a power over him he couldn't explain. What would happen if he was to have sex with her? Open himself up to her like that? A kiss was a means to an end, but that wasn't the case with Helia. Did he really want to risk flaying himself like that? Because he knew sex with her would be different. If a kiss could feel divine, sleeping with her would not be just a physical act. He couldn't allow it.

But the chemistry they had couldn't be ignored. It buzzed under his skin even now. They needed an outlet for it somehow. A way they could indulge without getting too close.

What about the fact that he wanted the monarchy to end with him, yet he was required to produce heirs with Helia? An heir and a spare—just like him. Perpetuating the same toxicity he had experienced with his own flesh and blood. Children. Innocents who would never have asked for this world.

He didn't really know what Helia wanted either—only what she'd agreed to. He didn't know whether she wanted children or not, and this life was certainly not going to give her a choice in the matter.

Concern for his people might have taken the choice of abdication away from him, but that didn't mean he had to ensure that the throne endured. It would end with him. Yes, he had married, as was required of him, and since this role of second-best ruler was what he'd been born for, he was now King. However, he could choose not to have children. It would be easy enough to control that.

Vasili crossed the room to a table that held a crystal decanter filled with amber liquid. He poured a measure into a glass and took a sip, relishing the burn in his throat.

He was resolute that he would not have any children just to have them forced into the life he lived. No one should have to suffer his fate...the fate of the King who shouldn't have been. And now he was expected to move into the King's quarters. He detested the idea but, thanks to tradition, he didn't have a choice. He would have to deal with the ghosts of that room. A room meant for his father and his brother but never him. Just the same as the role of King.

He would have to share these walls with people who had never seen the value in him. Who had always found him lacking. Bitter, awful people, who hadn't ever been happy, hadn't known love—who had held him in such disregard even though all he had ever wanted was to live his own life. Not to be placed aside just in case he was needed.

So he had lived in spite of them. The sex and the parties... they were all part of a life lived as hard as possible. But now that had to be put behind him. Now he had to look out for the people of this kingdom. People who probably wished that it had been him and not Leander on that plane.

He could feel it even within the palace walls. In the words Andreas said and in the silences he held. Perhaps it would have been simpler if it *had* been him. Nothing would have changed then. It would have meant little for Thalonia.

Vasili drained his glass and placed it on the towering stack of books on his bedside table.

Running his fingers through his hair, he realised these thoughts would get him nowhere. What he needed to do was decide how he would take on this new life. He had made a commitment to Helia.

Simply thinking her name had him wondering what she would be doing now, in that large room by herself. Wondering if she was upset or hurt. God, she was beautiful. She was his queen, and he would have to help her navigate this life, but she would in turn have to understand what their marriage would and wouldn't be.

Perhaps he should have discussed it with her before their marriage, but he hadn't known then just how much she could affect him.

That damn kiss!

He needed to talk to her, but he couldn't do it now. A night away from her was a good idea, but tomorrow they would forge a new path. One that he carved out.

Helia watched the door close in disbelief. She hadn't really known what to expect after the ceremonies. Of course she had been told what *should* happen. That she and Vasili should retire to their rooms with the unspoken expectation that they would consummate their marriage.

While Thalonian royals of eras long past had had separate quarters, that wasn't a practice followed by modern-day rulers, and certainly wasn't an option for them. Because they had to sell the image of a strong union which meant sharing a room.

She hadn't considered that Vasili would leave her standing there in her wedding dress immediately afterwards, as if he couldn't stand to be in her presence any longer. And it made her feel alone. A feeling she'd thought she was used to.

Helia tried to squash the hurt that needled at her.

What did you expect? Helia quietly chastised herself. Vasili had been honest about not wanting to be married. Just because they were in this together, it did not mean that would change.

Heaving a deep sigh, she bundled the long train of her wedding dress in her arms and walked into the bedroom, hoping to find something there to change into. A stunning white chemise was laid out on the bed. She ran her fingers over the delicate fabric but then snatched them back. She had no reason to wear such a garment.

She turned her back on it and marched into the large bathroom, where she found a thick robe.

With some difficulty Helia managed to get out of her wedding dress. She reached for the dressing gown, but stopped short of taking it off the hook. It was her wedding day and, while it might not have been the day she had dreamed of, why shouldn't she enjoy what came with it? She might have a reluctant groom, but he wasn't here now, and all indications were that she wouldn't see him again that day. She would never have been able to afford such a fine item before becoming Queen, so she marched back into the bedroom and slipped the chemise over her head, luxuriating in the way the fabric kissed her skin as it slid down her body.

She sat on the edge of the bed, taking the fabric between her fingers. There would be a lot to get used to now. Not least of all a husband who had little interest in her despite her attraction to him. That kiss during the ceremony had taken her by surprise. She had anticipated that Vasili might try to avoid it, or perhaps give her a peck on the cheek. But that kiss… It had robbed her of breath and clouded her mind. She had been intoxicated by his presence. His scent. The feel and taste of him. She had forgotten where they stood, giving in to the liquid heat consuming her.

If she closed her eyes, she could feel the phantom warmth from his fingers still ghosting across her cheek. She could have sworn that his eyes had darkened. That he'd been as breathless as her. But then she remembered it was she who was attracted to him. Any feelings from that kiss had been one-sided. After all, she had been the one to notice a hand-some prince…he had never noticed an invisible librarian…

Until he did.

Vasili was simply playing a part. As much as she thought she might possibly grow to love him, there was no good outcome to losing her heart to Vasili. She could allow her-self to enjoy his touches, but she had to remember it was all a show. Because he would not be married to her if he had been given a choice.

Would he ever have noticed her if she hadn't been in the library that day? What if one of the library assistants had been there instead of her? Would they be sitting in this room now? She suspected she knew the answer to that. After all, she was not good enough for the Prince who was now King. No one in the palace seemed to think she would be an adequate queen.

Helia ripped the tiara from her hair and tossed it upon

the dresser. Had she made a mistake? Or was she just letting the fact that Vasili had walked out unsettle her?

He's not the reason you're doing this, she reminded herself.

But she had to acknowledge that that was only half true. Her attraction to him was part of the reason, but the biggest part was that she would finally achieve her goal. Helping people like her was something she had always wanted to do, and she had vowed to find a way one day. Well, one day was here. She had chosen this union with her eyes open in order to serve her wants. So she would not second-guess herself simply because her husband needed space.

And it was obvious that he did.

From the moment the coronation ceremony had commenced Vasili had become withdrawn. There had been a haunted look in his eyes when he'd helped her out of the carriage that he hadn't been able to cover up in time. What if it wasn't just her but also this place that he'd needed to leave so urgently?

Helia had seen that he understood her addition to the vows, but maybe he needed to know that she would be on his side. This marriage needn't be a trap to make him miserable.

She would give him tonight, but tomorrow they would find a way to turn the crown into something they could both live with.

CHAPTER FIVE

THE SUN HAD barely risen. There would be little sign of life in the palace. But Vasili was already fixing the cufflinks on his shirt and pulling on his coat. He had contemplated his next move for most of the night. There were things that had to be done that neither he nor Helia could change, but he had to think bigger than just the next steps. Ground rules had to be outlined for their marriage. Boundaries neither of them would break. It was the best course of action for both of them.

First, he would have to apologise for his abrupt departure after the wedding. It had not been his finest moment, but Vasili was glad he had taken the time to sort through his thoughts.

Picking up his phone, Vasili called down to the kitchen. The one place that would already be hard at work.

'We will not be eating in the dining hall. Have breakfast sent to the room,' he instructed, not having to clarify which room he meant. He was supposed to have spent the night with his new wife. No one knew that he had instead spent the time in this room.

Hiding out.

He banished the thought. He wasn't hiding. He was strategising.

He had no idea how Helia would react, and hoped a

calm chat over breakfast in private would lead to her easy acquiescence.

With that thought Vasili left his room and made his way through the quiet halls to the King's room. *His* room.

He knocked twice and turned the knob, expecting that Helia would likely still be in bed given the hour. But when he entered he found her hurriedly shrugging on a satin peignoir.

As quickly as she tried to cinch the belt around her waist, Vasili still caught sight of the gossamer fabric of her chemise beneath. Arousal flared bright in his gut. All thought had been wiped from his mind save one: to kiss her. The blush creeping up her neck did nothing to quash his reaction. He wanted to peel that peignoir away. To see how far that blush travelled. Kiss her again like he'd done at the altar, but this time find out where that road would lead.

Vasili had slept badly, and when he had, he had dreamt of her. In his arms. In his room. For just a second his will-power to keep her at a distance wavered. He could show her such pleasure. He wanted to know more about her. Was desperate to. That desperation broke through the haze of want. Getting to know her, being intimate with her, exposing himself to her, was forbidden.

No one wants you like that. She *wouldn't want you like that.*

Of course she wouldn't. That was why he couldn't give her any reason to think they could be a normal married couple. They weren't. Not by any stretch of the imagination. More than that, he couldn't let her think that they could fall in love. Because he didn't love, had never been loved. It wasn't in his genetic make-up.

That didn't mean they needed to live a life without passion.

Vasili cleared his throat. 'I'm glad you're awake. We have a lot to talk about.'

'Good morning to you too, Your Majesty,' Helia sniped.

He had to bite his cheek to stop himself smiling. Either Helia was still upset by his hasty exit the day before or she was not a morning person. Perhaps both. It was an idea he found oddly endearing and he filed the information away.

'Good morning, Helia. Did you sleep well?' Try as he might, he couldn't hide his amusement.

'Marvellously, thank you.'

'I've taken the liberty of sending for breakfast.'

As if it had been planned, a knock sounded at the door. 'That will be it right now.'

He opened the door and stood aside as a servant wheeled in a trolley with several cloches sitting on top.

He greeted Helia and Vasili with a bow, and was about to serve the new King and Queen when Vasili stopped him with a smile.

'That's all right, we can handle it from here.'

He closed the door, then pushed the trolley towards the small table in the room and went about lifting the lids before taking his seat and pouring two cups of coffee.

'Join me?'

Vasili might not have had the same level of rigorous training to be King as his brother, but he did know that he needed different approaches to win different people over. Sometimes a blatant show of power was needed, but at other times a softer touch was more effective. Given Helia's irascible mood, and the subject at hand, he knew he would need to be amiable. Charm her. And that was something he could do effortlessly.

He handed one of the cups to her, noting that she added

neither cream nor sugar before taking a sip of the steaming hot drink.

'Pancakes?' he asked.

He watched Helia study him closely before she answered. 'Yes, please.'

He loaded her plate with pancakes, cream and fresh berries, before serving himself the same. If what he wanted to speak to her about hadn't been so important, he would have laughed at her confusion.

He watched her drain her cup before starting on the pancakes. If he was going to have a civilised conversation about their way forward, now was the time.

'Helia, I would like to apologise for my behaviour yesterday. Both at the wedding and after. I shouldn't have kissed you and I most certainly should not have left the way I did.'

'Why did you leave?'

She seemed focused on cutting up her food. Her calm indifference had to be an act. Still, he was glad they had a distraction of sorts for this conversation.

He picked up his utensils. 'I needed to think. The situation we find ourselves in is not an easy one to navigate, so we need to set some ground rules. Discuss our expectations.'

'Go on.'

'I know you have been told that in agreeing to be Queen you will be expected to bear heirs to the throne.'

Helia's cautious gaze landed on him. 'I have.'

'I don't want you to be concerned about that. I do not expect a physical relationship. You will not bear us any heirs. We will not have sex.'

After that kiss, he couldn't take the risk. He needed this boundary for himself.

Vasili waited for his words to land. Watched her stiffen as she speared a strawberry.

'Would it not have been prudent to mention this to me before we were married, Your Majesty?' she snapped.

'Your Majesty?' Vasili repeated, taken aback by the sharpness of her tone.

'Seems appropriate, given how you are dictating to me. And what about the crown?'

Her fork clattered on the plate as she placed her hands on the table. Vasili noticed how she forced herself to flatten her palms on the tablecloth as they tried to curl into fists.

'It will end with me.'

Regardless of whatever Helia said next, he would not budge on this. He had decided he would not have children, and nothing would change his mind.

'Do you want children?' he asked. He had to know, because if she did, all of this would have to end right now.

'I don't know. I hadn't had the luxury of thinking about the possibility all that much until two weeks ago, when I was *told* I would be expected to, and now again I am being *told* that I won't. It's my body, and possibly my family, but clearly I don't get a say in this decision?'

She was right, so he couldn't blame her for being angry.

'Are we still being honest?' she asked, after taking a breath, but he could still hear her temper in her voice.

'Always.'

'Then why? Help me understand.'

'I will not have an heir and a spare. It is my mission to move this kingdom to a system of governance that will never again require a royal.'

'You really hate it.'

'I do.'

'And yet you're willing to do the duty you hate for the people you are now responsible for.'

The fire had gone out of her tone.

'What's your point?'

There was a shimmer of emotion in her eyes that she blinked away. He could see there were more questions she wanted to ask.

Helia shook her head. 'It doesn't matter. Not at this moment at least. But I need to understand a few things.'

'Of course.'

'You are aware of your reputation. I have seen all the women you entertain, Vasili. If I am not the one in your bed, and if you are choosing not to have heirs—children— what does that mean?'

That tension she had managed to let go of earlier was back in her shoulders. He supposed he had earned his play-boy reputation and could understand her concern over the potential embarrassment she would suffer.

'Are you asking me if I will stray?'

His voice had dropped an octave. He didn't like her calling his integrity into question. He knew his reaction was unfounded, because he had chosen the path his life had taken, but he would never deliberately hurt anyone. Especially not Helia.

'I am. If I am to be Queen—'

'You *are* Queen.'

She stared him down and continued, despite his interruption. 'I will not be embarrassed by a scandal. My goals are too important to endanger them like that.'

Vasili placed his knife and fork on his plate and pushed it aside, clasping his hands on the table as he leaned towards her. 'I will not be unfaithful to you, Helia.' She looked down at her plate, but he needed her to understand. 'Look at me,' he demanded. 'I may not have wanted to marry, but I did make a promise to you. Despite what might be said about me, I am a man of my word.'

'But—'

'But nothing. I am well aware of my reputation, but what you need to understand is that I have never wanted to be a royal.'

It looked as if Helia wanted to interrupt, but he wouldn't let her.

'We agreed on honesty from the start, so that is what you're going to get. I am sure you have noticed that I tend to rebel against this institution...' He waved his hands through the air, to indicate the palace and everything in it. Helia smiled, as if to say obviously she'd noticed. 'My philandering was nothing more than rebellion against how I was supposed to act as Prince. And it was effective. But I don't need it. It was simply an act meant to serve me.'

'That may be...but never is a very long time, Vasili. To say that you won't miss the company of women or won't want children...'

'I can say that I won't want children, and I am not saying I will have no company. There is chemistry between us Helia, I'm certain you feel it.'

He could tell by the way she swallowed that she did. It was impossible not to.

'What I am proposing is a marriage with no sex, but one in which we explore this thing between us. One with passion and pleasure. Helia, I will never love you—I am not capable of it—but I will remain faithful to you and expect the same from you. This marriage isn't about love. It's about duty. But why should we deprive ourselves because of it? However, you have to make the choice.'

* * *

Helia was dumbstruck. It irked her that he was dictating to her, but the truth of the matter was that she was married to Vasili. She doubted anyone else would turn her head ever again. Besides him, no one had since her first and only relationship.

She didn't understand why he would want passion without sex. It had been a big part of his life before. Was it her? Was this some sort of unfortunate attraction for him and he didn't truly want her?

Helia didn't want to admit how much that stung, but she was a realist, and just because she was extremely attracted to him it didn't mean he had to reciprocate. But to go through a whole life without love would be lonely. Especially without children. Without family.

Except she hadn't had love since she was orphaned, and she had survived. Why did she think her life now would be any different? Besides, it wasn't as if she would be without distraction. The prospect of experiencing pleasure at the hands of Vasili was exciting. So exciting, in fact, that her thighs squeezed together under the table.

So maybe she would be lonely, but she would also have passion unlike anything she had ever experienced.

And maybe it was a blessing that he was so set against having heirs. It was by far a better choice than having children he didn't want and would regret having. Children who might possibly be abandoned or bear the emotional scars of not being wanted—or, worse, children who would be left alone if something were to happen to her and Vasili.

But could he really manage a lifetime without sex?

'Tell me what you're thinking,' he said.

Helia wasn't sure she wanted to. It was evident that Vasili

had had to deal with a lot of doubt when it came to who he was and what he could do, so she didn't want to speak hers aloud and add to the voices.

'Tell me,' Vasili insisted.

'I don't know if you would be able to turn off such a big part of yourself. You admitted that was who you had to be for a long time, and it doesn't seem possible to me for you to just switch off those urges.'

'If it was that important to me we wouldn't be having this discussion now. I would do as I pleased. As I have always done. I don't need it, Helia.'

Helia thought about it. His words didn't feel much like reassurance at all. And there was still the issue of children. She hadn't thought about having her own. Not when all her life she had been focused on surviving. When she had been alone. She hadn't even thought about children when she was in a relationship, and that had been doomed to fail.

'I need time to think about it,' she said.

'About what?'

'All of it.'

'Fine. I will give it to you.' Vasili sat back in his chair and took a sip of his now cooled coffee. 'We will have to make a public appearance—our first official appearance—when we return from our honeymoon.'

'Honeymoon?'

That caught Helia off guard. She hadn't known there would be one, but she realised she had been ridiculous not to think of it. Naturally there would have to be, for appearances' sake.

'Yes, Helia, a honeymoon. You can take all the time you need to consider what we have discussed here while we are away. I know what it is I have just proposed, and we will not be physical in any way until you come to a decision.'

He placed his cup down and in a gentler voice said, 'I think we both need to come to terms with all that has changed.'

He was right. She definitely did.

'When do we leave?' she asked.

'Today.'

She nodded, not bothering to ask where they were going. It didn't really matter.

'Now, about our first appearance... I want you to pick what we do. I realise it will take you some time to get used to your new life, so choose something that will make you comfortable and Andreas will arrange it.'

'Andreas will arrange something *I* choose?' Helia challenged with a cocked brow. She stopped short of scoffing.

'Yes, he will. Need I remind you there was a coronation yesterday? You are Queen. You have power. Use it. And should you need it, I will support you.'

There was a look she couldn't decipher that passed over his face, but she appreciated the words, nonetheless. 'Thank you.'

'That's what a husband is for.'

Despite all that they'd spoken of, Helia laughed. 'Is it?'

'So I hear. Other things include reminding their wives about unpleasant events—like the coronation banquet that will be held a few weeks after we return.'

She could tell he was trying to keep the atmosphere light, but the tic in his jaw and the fact that his smile hadn't reached his eyes betrayed his true feelings.

'Why does that bother you so much?'

Vasili studied her intently before heaving a deep sigh, as if the weight of the world sat upon his shoulders. She supposed it did.

'It sickens me that Leander died only two weeks ago and yet now a banquet is being planned. We've had a celebration in the city. It just…' He took in a deep breath and glanced out of the window, grasping the armrests of his chair.

Helia understood. Vasili was grieving more than anyone realised or cared to acknowledge. Yes, the Kingdom had lost its king, but now it had a new one. Vasili had lost his brother. His flesh and blood. Not a title or someone who could be replaced.

'Vasili,' she said gently. She wanted to take his hand in hers but refrained from doing so. He was looking at her, and that would have to be enough. 'I know this marriage isn't what you chose, but I meant my vows. I will support you. This union between us can be what we make it, and if you want to postpone the banquet then that is what we'll do. If you want to have a ceremony to honour Leander instead, we'll do that. You have lost your brother, and you should do what you need to be free of all the chains your advisors have wrapped around you. So, tell me what you need and I will help you make it happen.'

'Helia…'

Her name was a breath on his lips. He said nothing else as he stared at her. Whatever emotion was contained in that one word was not reflected on his blank face.

It was clear Vasili had loved his brother deeply. And he cared about so much that he wouldn't reveal. He was willing to do something he truly hated because he cared about his people. If there was anyone who would support her goal it was him. And she felt her silly heart give up a piece of itself to the King.

'Get dressed, Helia. We will leave shortly.'

His voice had grown low.

Helia nodded and closed the door to the bedroom behind her, feeling utterly devastated for him.

CHAPTER SIX

HELIA FOUND HERSELF in the King's office. Vasili's office.

After their chat over breakfast, she'd readied herself as quickly as possible in clothes she didn't recognise and made her way with Vasili to this room. It didn't suit him at all. Everything seemed to have been carefully chosen to project an image of modernity, but without pushing the boundaries of tradition. That wasn't Vasili. Since she had first seen him, everything he had done had smashed down tradition's stifling walls. He didn't toe any line. He challenged it. It felt as if everything here had been designed for someone else and Vasili was the understudy that didn't fit.

The notion angered her.

'I thought we were meeting with Andreas,' she said, turning away from the fresco she had been examining.

'We are, but we're making him come to us. In fact… Would you come over here, Helia?'

Without thinking, she obeyed, walking over to Vasili, who had pulled his chair out.

'Have a seat.'

Helia stopped short. It might not be the throne, but that was most certainly the King's seat. Arguably the most important seat in the Kingdom. And he was offering it to her.

'I couldn't possibly.'

'Of course you could.'

He waited. Clearly he wouldn't back down.

Helia's heart thumped in her chest. She didn't know what to make of this. She sat down and he pushed the chair in, then rounded the table to face her.

'You look good there, Your Majesty.'

'Vasili, don't tease.' Obviously it was all in her head, but the chair, the table, this whole office, suddenly felt far too big for her.

'I'm not. Here are a few things to remember, Helia. Firstly, always make them come to you. Especially Andreas. Use my office or your own—it doesn't matter. Never go to them. Secondly, you're the Queen of Thalonia. The title might chafe, but it brings power. Wield it.'

'It's not that easy,' she admitted.

'No, it isn't. I understand this is all overwhelming, and that everyone here might seem as if they know more than you do, and that's fine. Learn from them, but don't ever let them forget who they're talking to.'

She understood what he was doing. In giving her his chair, Vasili was establishing the power balance between her and his closest advisor. Gratitude clogged her throat. But there was no time to express it because there was a knock at the door. Vasili held her gaze a moment longer, then turned around and perched on the edge of the table.

Andreas's attitude generally frustrated her, so she watched with some satisfaction as he entered the room and stopped in his tracks when he caught sight of them. The older man's brows knitted together, and for the first time she was glad for the change in her wardrobe. She doubted this would be nearly as effective if she had still been dressed like a librarian.

'Your Majesties.' Andreas inclined his head as he sketched a small bow.

'Andreas,' Vasili said. The authority in his voice was impressive. 'Have a seat.'

Helia watched him sit down in the chair opposite, casting a cursory glance her way before fixing his attention on the King.

'We wish to speak to you about the public appearance to be held once we return from our honeymoon.' He didn't take his eyes off Andreas. 'Helia, why don't you tell him what we have decided?'

She knew she needed to pass this initial test by wielding her power with a man who still attempted to intimidate her. She hoped her nervousness wouldn't show in her voice.

'Our first outing will be to the Seidon orphanage. We will meet with the caregivers there and the children. In that meeting we are going to find out exactly how the home is run, what help they need, and then work on measures to help.'

With every word she could see Andreas growing more and more unimpressed, until he could no longer keep his opinions leashed.

'Absolutely not.'

'I'm sorry?' replied Helia, afraid that her idea was going to die in this room.

Andreas took his time answering. No doubt choosing his words as diplomatically as possible. 'As admirable as your intentions may be, that is not an appropriate choice for your first sighting as King and Queen. The point is to introduce you both to the Kingdom and the world—because make no mistake the world will be watching—and show you in the best possible light. Not doing something that will take the focus away from you. We don't want the first thing we put on show to be—'

'Our country's failures? Should we hide everything that's wrong so that it will make everyone look good?' Helia challenged.

She knew she needed to be calm—she felt anything but. Her voice had risen as anger had coursed through her. Men like Andreas were the reason she and the other children had been cold in winter. Why they'd had to make do with what little they'd had.

Andreas didn't even look slightly uncomfortable. 'Every kingdom has its issues. It's an unfortunate reality.'

'Issues?' Helia exclaimed in disbelief. She was certain that this was not how a queen should behave, but she couldn't stop herself now. 'We need to do something about it.'

She could see the battle she would be facing to have her goals met. With Vasili having accepted his duty purely for the concern of his people, she reasoned that he would be on her side in her quest, but getting everyone else to play their part would be a fight.

'Eventually we may be able to look into it.'

A non-committal answer if ever there was one.

'We need to look at more appropriate public appearances and I am happy to help you with that.'

'What is more appropriate than showing an interest in helping the children of Thalonia? Where will this kingdom be without them? You are determined to secure the future of our nation, so surely this fits in with that objective?'

Gone was the quiet librarian. Right now, in this office, she would fight with all she had for her people.

Andreas had gone tense with frustration. 'I didn't say we wouldn't do anything about it, only that we need to choose wisely for your first public appearance. We have numerous options available to us. There is a charity concert being held by the symphonic orchestra. That would resonate well, as previous kings and queens have often chosen the same event. It will show the people that you are willing to uphold our traditions despite your history.'

Helia didn't miss the jab, but Andreas ploughed on.

'There is the annual polo match—or even a charity ball. Any of those would work well. Which should I arrange?'

Rage. That was what burned through Helia now. Andreas assumed that she would back down and listen. She wouldn't.

Just as she was about to argue, Vasili spoke. His voice was calm, but no one would dare oppose his tone. It would be enough to silence Andreas.

'That's enough. We brought you here to inform you of our decision. Your queen has given her orders. We are going to the orphanage.'

'My apologies, Your Majesty,' he said rigidly. 'It shall be arranged.'

'Good.'

Andreas swiftly exited the office, leaving Helia alone with Vasili. He had been so opposed it concerned her that he wouldn't plan the appearance.

'Do you think he will follow through?' Helia asked, feeling ashamed that she had reacted so strongly. She had let Andreas control her emotions instead of being the one in control. She had failed her very first test.

'Yes. Andreas may not be happy with the situation, but serving the royal family is something for which he holds a great deal of pride. Regardless of his opinions, he will do as he is ordered.'

Helia hoped so, but she wasn't given much time to brood

over the matter when Vasili appeared at her side, offering her his hand.

'Come, we have to leave.'

She placed her hand in his, ignoring the flutter in her belly, and allowed him to lead her through the palace and out to the expansive gardens at the rear, where a gleaming red helicopter waited. She was debating whether or not she should apologise.

The rotors swished as they approached, quickly gathering speed and creating an almighty wind. Goosebumps erupted on her skin when Vasili's hand came up to her nape, forcing her thoughts away and making her bend slightly to see a man in a black suit with an earpiece standing at the door.

'Why are we travelling by helicopter?' she asked loudly, so he could hear her over the din.

She waited for an answer that only came after he had helped her inside, ushering her into one of four cream leather seats.

'Because, Helia, only two of our security detail can travel with us,' he said as he buckled her into the harness.

The touches made it hard for her to pay any attention to his words.

'I figured you would be far more comfortable alone with me than an entire entourage.' His eyes flicked to hers.

She was at a loss for words. Vasili hadn't wanted to be married, or to be King, yet he continued to show her more consideration than anyone else. If she wasn't meant to love him, his actions would make that very difficult. How was she supposed to keep her emotions out of a physical relationship if he was to treat her with such kindness?

She couldn't trust herself to keep to that promise if she had to make it. Did it mean she would have to keep her distance? She couldn't see another way to ensure that she would never fall in love with him. To mitigate the risk of that ever happening.

After all, her plans depended on her remaining as Queen, so she would have to agree to Vasili's emotionless marriage.

Some honeymoon this would be.

'You're right. Thank you,' she said now.

'Are you nervous?' Vasili asked as he strapped himself in.

'A little. I've never flown before,' she admitted.

More and more she was coming to realise how out of her depth she was in this life.

The flight took barely over an hour, and in that time she couldn't tear her gaze away from the scenery around them.

It was Thalonia as she had never seen it before.

The turquoise waters of the Ionian Sea glittered as if it was covered in jewels. The city gave way to beaches and cliffs and dense green forests.

The only thing that challenged the view was Vasili's presence. She kept stealing glances at the King, who had a faraway look in his eyes.

He caught her staring, and she knew she should look away, but she couldn't. There was something unreadable in that intense gaze. It almost seemed as if he couldn't look away either. A muscle in his jaw flexed. They were stuck in this world where beauty existed all around them but had faded to nothing.

It was the slight bump of the helicopter touching down that wrenched them away.

Vasili exited first, silently helping Helia out afterwards, and, with a hand on her back and her heart thumping furiously at his touch he guided her away from the aircraft.

She paid no attention to where she was being led because, to her, they had arrived in Paradise.

Protected by steep cliffs on all sides, the resort was a hidden gem, with only a few white chalets. She heard Vasili say something, but couldn't make out the words as they stepped onto a wooden pathway that was flanked by all sorts of plants, winding between each chalet. They were spaced so far apart they would have complete privacy. And as they walked forward she saw a private beach emerge, with pristine shore and clear waters. She noticed each pathway emerged onto the sand, like a delta meeting the sea.

'Leave us,' she heard Vasili say, and turned around to find their security detail disappearing off onto another path.

She looked to Vasili, who answered her question before she could ask it.

'They will be staying on site in the furthest chalet from ours. No one is here, Helia. Apart from the resort staff, we're alone.'

For days on end she would have only Vasili for company.

A thrill of excitement shot through her at the prospect. But so did trepidation, and a little loneliness, at knowing she had to keep away from him.

She stepped inside the chalet and had to pinch herself to remind her that now she spent her time in places like this.

The chalet was by far the most luxurious place she had ever seen. Her old apartment could have fitted in it many times over with space to spare. It was large and airy, with fluttering gauzy curtains hanging at windows and archways. She flitted from room to room. There was so much light, so many openings to the outside, that it barely seemed they were indoors at all.

And then she spotted a set of doors that undoubtedly led to the bedroom. Helia rushed through, but was drawn short. Not by the spectacular views, of which this particular chalet must have the best one, nor by the plunge pool that could be stepped into right from the bedroom itself, despite there being an enormous swimming pool out on the deck, but by the bed.

The very large, very singular bed.

Helia's excitement morphed into anxiety as she remembered their talk. She hadn't yet agreed to his terms and he had promised they would not be physical in any way until she did. But how would she be able to think, to keep her distance, if she was in the same bed as him?

She knew she had to while they were on this honeymoon, but she couldn't help wonder what it would be like to share a bed with him. Did Vasili even want to?

She searched around the room, hoping for some sort of solution to magically make itself known. There was a chaise in the room, and several couches in the living area, one of which would be large enough to sleep on should things become awkward. But she couldn't tell the King not to sleep on the bed. Especially not when they should be on their honeymoon.

Helia supposed she was small enough that she could comfortably sleep there. If there were staff in the grounds, their sleeping in different chalets was not an option—just as it wasn't an option at the palace. They were the newly married King and Queen and they had to keep up appearances.

'You look uncomfortable.'

Helia jumped at the deep, raspy voice behind her. She hadn't heard Vasili enter.

'Did I startle you?'

'No.'

She didn't need to see his face to know that he didn't

believe her lie. His sharply exhaled breath did that more than adequately.

'I can sleep elsewhere, Helia. Relax.'

His voice had come from above her head, but it was his heat at her back that she felt most intensely. She would have loved nothing more than to lean into that. See if his embrace would ignite her like his kiss had, or if his immoveable hardness would comfort her.

But that was not the marriage they had, and she had to remember that fact.

'I can't let you do that.'

She took a few steps away from him. Distance was what she needed, or she knew she would want to savour his very presence.

'You'll find there's very little that anyone can forbid me from doing.'

'I get that you're the King, Vasili. But I also very much doubt you would fit on that couch.'

His lips twitched as if he was battling a smile. She didn't see what was so funny. This was an impossible situation. There was no way she would let him be uncomfortable for the entirety of their stay. And what if the staff entered to find one of them sleeping on the couch? They were definitely on hand. As discreet as she was sure they were, gossip would get out, and all the hard work they were doing—had already done to ensure everyone believed the monarchy stood strong—would be undone.

There was just no way around this.

'I appreciate you thinking of my comfort,' he said. 'But I didn't say I would sleep on the couch.'

It took her a moment to understand his words. 'But you can't sleep elsewhere. What happens if the staff notice? Or a picture gets out? We can't afford the gossip. *I* can't afford the gossip.'

'We'll handle it,' he said gruffly.

'I refuse to give anyone ammunition to use against me. Most of your advisors are already against my being Queen. My goals are too important to jeopardise. Look, I know what we agreed to, but we're going to be sharing a bed in the palace anyway.'

She could see him thinking it through. He looked as if he wanted to say no. Did he think sharing with her would be so bad? she wondered.

'Are you certain you are prepared for that?'

'Yes,' she lied.

He didn't look as if he believed her.

'Very well,' he said stiffly.

Helia couldn't get a read on him. Only knew that he was far more tense than he had been at any point during the day so far—including when he had strapped her into the helicopter seat. Perhaps an escape would do them both good.

'I'm going for a walk.'

She hoped the sea air would settle all her conflicting feelings.

Helia returned to the chalet after dark, having had time to process what the week might possibly be like. Vasili was nowhere to be found, so she ordered room service, which she enjoyed on her own, and then readied herself for bed.

She wheeled her suitcase into the bathroom, cursing as she pawed through it. Her earlier gratitude for having her wardrobe changed had vanished, and was now replaced with mortification. She had already come to terms with the fact that her own wardrobe was not fit for royalty, but surely her nightwear didn't have to be collateral damage in this war on her identity. No one would ever see her in it.

Unfortunately, as she picked through everything that

had been packed for her, she found nothing that she would have chosen for herself. No comfy yoga pants or soft shirts.

Every negligee was more flimsy or weblike than the last. She could appreciate the beauty of them, the luxurious feel of the fabric, but how could she wear something like these without Vasili thinking that she was accepting his terms when she hadn't yet come to a decision?

Helia put on what she thought to be the most modest of the lot. The deep red satin was vivid against her olive skin, but at least it covered her up.

She shut off the light and stepped back into the bedroom to find Vasili already in bed. He was sitting against the headboard, shirtless, paying no mind to her as he read something on his phone.

She had felt the hardness of his body, had seen the way he moved with a powerful grace, but she was still not prepared for the vision of his naked chest, which looked as if it had been carved from stone. The sculpted, shadowed dips and peaks of his stomach were highlighted by the lamplight. The bedcovers were tossed carelessly around his hips, and she could just make out the band of his underwear.

She couldn't take her eyes off him. Vasili was glorious.

Her heart gave a sharp throb, and she realised that she had been staring.

She forced herself to move and, as carefully as she could, slunk towards the bed, slowly climbing beneath the covers to avoid catching his attention. She settled as close to the edge as possible, trying exceptionally hard to ignore the fact that she was now sharing a bed with the man she was impossibly attracted to but from whom she was determined to keep her distance.

'You're going to fall out of the bed. Come closer.'

When she didn't listen, Vasili dropped his phone onto

the duvet and reached around her, pulling her away from the edge. The touch scalded him to his core. His body rejoiced at her nearness.

He hadn't been able to concentrate on a single word in the email he had been reading. How could he have been expected to concentrate when he had felt Helia's gaze dragging across his body like a touch? How could his every nerve not have been attuned to her when she'd walked out of that bathroom looking like an enticing dream? If the people of Thalonia had still believed in mythological deities, she would undoubtedly have been one.

He tried not looking at her, hoping that would be enough to wrangle the arousal coursing through him into submission. He had to control himself. He would not make this any more uncomfortable for her than it already was. Helia had agreed to this marriage without being given much of a choice, and to him that was no consent at all.

Which was why he had said there would be no physical relationship. No matter how much he wanted to slip his hand under all that satin, explore her body... It was the very reason he wanted to sleep away from her—he couldn't allow it.

He took a breath to master himself. Not that it helped much when he could smell her floral fragrance and wondered if she would smell that sweet everywhere.

Helia was embedded in his mind, and she wasn't going anywhere soon. He had wanted to bow down to her in his office. She had been regal in that chair, and more than that he had been proud of the way she had handled Andreas. He had wanted to kiss her afterwards, and even though he'd managed to hold back, there had been no reprieve.

Buckling her into her seat in the helicopter had been another test he hadn't felt prepared for. To be so close to her. To touch her and feel every contact like a white-hot shock. That flight had seemed like the longest he had ever taken. Every minute had been spent figuring out a way that he could either avoid Helia on their honeymoon or how he could get a taste of her without getting close. And then she had looked at him. Trapped him in a bubble that silenced the world. Quieted his anxiety.

And now, as if all of that had not been enough for one day, there was the bed.

When she had suggested that they share, Vasili had wondered if there would ever be a point in his life when the universe wouldn't answer him with cruelty. He didn't want to sleep with Helia. He didn't want to let his guard down around her. To be vulnerable. There was no control in sleep. Nothing to stop warm embraces. No shields to stop them gravitating towards each other.

It had been test upon test, and he felt as if he was failing miserably because he simply could not contain this chemistry between them.

He had kissed her once and it had given her some sort of power over him. He couldn't allow it—which was why he wanted to enforce the boundaries in their marriage. That was the end of it. No matter how badly he wanted a taste, Vasili refused to give in.

'Go to sleep, Helia.' He reached over and flicked the light switch.

'Goodnight, Vasili,' she replied in a barely-there whisper as the room was plunged into darkness.

If he'd thought the black night would allow them to relax, he couldn't have been more wrong. With nothing to focus on apart from the weight of each other in the bed, and their audible breaths, he felt the tension between them magnified by the dark until they could focus on nothing but each other.

Vasili's entire body was alert to the proximity of Helia.

He wanted so badly to reach out to her. She was so close. He felt her hand twitch against the sheets, but refused to allow himself to think of what it would be like if she crossed that small expanse between them.

He lay awake for hours, and knew Helia did too. They were keenly aware of each other, and of the mounting current in the air. Desire was like a fog, suspended around them, but neither would reach out. Vasili would not break his word to her or to himself.

There was a scraping against the sheets…a tug he felt.

Clearly Helia felt the same.

CHAPTER SEVEN

THE SOUND OF crashing water was the first thing Helia heard. Then she felt a warm weight around her body. Slowly, other sounds met the first. Chirping birds. Soft breaths. As Helia was roused, she took in more of her surroundings. She was in bed, with light pouring in from all the open doors and windows. She was lying on her back, and when she looked over she saw Vasili sound asleep. Lying on his side. One arm was under her, the other was over her stomach, holding her close. His leg was wrapped around hers.

She had no idea when they had ended up in this position. She had tried to keep a physical space between them, and had been so tense she hadn't thought she would fall asleep at all.

But she obviously had.

She turned slightly so she could get a good look at Vasili.

The King.

Her husband.

He was so beautiful. Dark, thick lashes fanned over his cheeks. His slightly curly hair fell in mussed waves. Fleshy pink lips were slightly parted. And then there was his body, which she could feel but couldn't see, because he held her so close.

She was warm in his embrace. Content. Helia savoured

this moment. A memory she would keep tucked away safely.

She had always wondered what it would be like to be held by him. Wondered what his lips might feel like. Even in those days spent in the library, when she had admired him from afar, she would let herself dream that one day he would see her. Would want to caress and kiss her. Now she'd had a taste of him. Knew what kissing him really felt like. And no imagination, no matter how creative, could have compared. Now she had an idea of what it would be like to wake up in his arms every morning, and a very significant part of her wished she could have more.

But she couldn't.

He would never be doing this if he was awake.

He wouldn't give that to her.

It was dangerous to think these thoughts. Dangerous for the goals that rested on her being the Queen Vasili needed, and especially dangerous for her heart. Only heartache awaited down that path. Because even though she was happy to be in his arms, it would feel even lonelier soon. When he woke and pulled away she would have to deal with that warmth abandoning her.

All these feelings told her that she was already struggling to separate the emotional from the physical. They had simply needed to sleep, but she was wishing for more.

Being in this bed wasn't doing her any favours. So, as carefully as she could, she slipped from his embrace and quietly went to the bathroom, where she changed as quickly as she could into a jade bikini, and threw a long beach kimono over it. The pattern reminded her of an antique vase.

She left the chalet and walked barefoot along the slatted wooden path until she stepped onto the beach. The sand was still cool beneath her feet, but she knew that wouldn't last long. Not with the summer sun that would beat down soon enough.

Helia walked all the way to the water's edge, where the warm water fizzed over her toes, catching the very edges of the kimono that fluttered around her ankles. She was utterly alone on the beach, and she felt a part of her settle in the peace. For two weeks, every day had been a rush—a constant hum of voices and activity. She had missed the tranquillity of the library but now, on this beach, where there wasn't another soul for miles, Helia found what she had been craving.

It had been quiet the night before, too, when Vasili had turned out the lights. Except that silence had been deafening. As loud as a scream. All she'd been able to feel in the dark was his presence. The want that coursed through her. The need to reach out and touch him.

When he had turned out the lights it had felt as if they had entered a void where there was no escape from her attraction to him. Where it had become a physical entity. There had been no distraction in the darkness. Nowhere to focus other than on herself and him.

Her nails had scraped against the sheets as she had fisted the linen, trying to stop herself doing something terrible like reaching for him. She had almost considered erecting a physical barrier between them. There were enough pillows in the room. But she'd known she couldn't do that and show Vasili how much he affected her.

Then she remembered how she'd woken up, and that felt like a dream itself.

She walked the length of the beach before turning around and walking back towards the resort. But she couldn't go back there yet and risk facing him. She dropped down onto the sand, hugging her knees as she gazed out at the water, pondering how much her life had changed.

It hadn't been that long ago when she'd wished she could see more of Thalonia. She'd earned a comfortable wage working at the palace. More than comfortable. But, as much as she'd wanted adventure, staying close to her books was safe. Books kept the loneliness at bay. Books couldn't be taken from her, wouldn't desert her.

The life Vasili was proposing would be a lonely one. She wanted to experience passion with him—of course she did—but how could she agree to never falling in love or never having children when she had no idea what the future might hold?

And now she was in a paradise she would never in her wildest dreams have been able to visit before, on a honeymoon that was simply a pause. Because once they returned to Seidon, Helia would have to fight to achieve her dream. Then it would no longer be a dream…would no longer be a niggle at the back of her mind, something she wished she could make happen. It would be reality.

Helia was lost to her thoughts as she stared out at the turquoise waters. Paying no attention to her surroundings, she heard nothing when someone stepped onto the sand, surprising her as she felt him sit beside her.

'Good morning, Helia,' Vasili said. His gaze was cast out over the sea as well. 'Did you sleep well?'

Not at all. But she couldn't admit to the reason.

'I did, thank you.'

'I always forget how beautiful it is out here.'

'Have you been here often?'

'Not as much recently.' He glanced over his shoulder at the resort. 'But a few times in the past.'

Of course he had. Helia's stomach sank as she imagined the kind of company he had come here with.

'It's a beautiful morning for a swim.'

'I don't think that's a very good idea.'

Not for her, at least. While it wasn't an invitation on his part, she needed to ensure that they spent as little time together as possible. And besides, swimming was never an option for her.

'Why not?'

She could feel him looking at her, so she turned towards him to give him an answer. It was another way in which she was lacking. Another simple skill that the Queen of Thalonia didn't have. And what an embarrassment that would be. Yet another way she was inadequate.

'I can't swim,' she said softly.

Shock crossed his face. 'How is that possible? We live on an island. The sea is in our blood.'

'I love the sea. There is a quiet little spot near the lighthouse where I go to be alone. It's my favourite place.' Helia could see the curiosity on his face. Turning back to the water, so he couldn't see the pain on hers, she continued. 'But I've never been in the water.'

'Ever?'

'Ever.'

The grief that often reared its head when she thought of her father smashed into her, but she had learnt how to keep it from showing to the people around her.

'My father owned a business and was always too busy to teach me how to swim. It wasn't something taught at our little school, and after he passed away I never had an opportunity to learn.'

It was as if a tidal wave of sorrow poured from Helia, even though Vasili could see that she was trying to hide her feelings. It made him want to pull her into his arms and protect her from this heartache that she carried around.

Vasili was fighting his curiosity about her. He shouldn't want to know more. What he learnt would make no difference to their strange relationship, no matter how much he lusted for her.

'What about your mother?' he asked.

She shook her head. 'I never knew her. She died when I was an infant.'

'So it was just you and your father?'

'Yes.'

Vasili had always felt alone, despite having a family, but Helia…she truly was alone. Well, not any more. Because his ring did sit on her finger, even if it was impossible for him to be the kind of husband she would want.

The way she looked at the water, with such longing, broke his heart. It was true that Vasili had to protect himself from Helia. To prevent her from getting too close. But he wouldn't let the situation they were in change the man he was—and that man would never be cruel enough to leave someone drowning in their grief. In their loneliness.

Like you are?

Standing up, he ignored that voice, holding out a hand to her instead. 'Come with me.'

She hesitated before placing her hand in his. 'Where are we going?'

'You'll see.'

He released her hand as soon as he'd pulled her up, leading her to the massive sparkling blue pool on the deck. He descended the steps one at a time, feeling the water rising with each step, until he was waist-deep, his feet planted firmly on the floor of the pool.

He turned back to Helia then, holding out his hand with an inviting smile. 'Join me.'

Vasili watched her closely as he waited at the wide steps.

Her eyes darted the length of the pool. Fixating on the deep end.

'Don't think about that yet. Just join me over here.'

Satisfaction and heat battled for dominance within him as he noticed the way her gaze travelled from his upturned palm to his body. She was drinking in every inch of his bare skin.

'Trust me.'

The two words had her gaze meeting his, and then, with a deep breath, she screwed up her courage, peeled off her kimono and slowly stepped into the water.

Pure pride washed through him, but he pushed that aside. Pride wasn't something he would allow himself to feel for this person he was trying to keep at arm's length.

Vasili moved towards her, and she latched on to his hand the moment he offered it.

'That's it,' he encouraged, leading her to the next step, and the next, until she was standing with him.

'How do you feel?' Vasili asked. He could see how tense she was.

'Okay for now.'

'Just breathe, Helia. The water is shallow. Relax.'

She nodded, but his heart twisted at seeing all her confidence vanish.

'I won't let anything happen to you.'

'I believe you,' she said, in a slightly tremulous voice.

Her beauty paralysed him. Vasili stood in the water with her, taking in the way her swimsuit covered her up but left little to the imagination. As bikinis went, it was modest. Vasili had been on boats with women who wore far less. Yet this green garment had him in a chokehold. It revealed just enough of her breasts for him to picture kissing them.

Leaving his mark on them. Her bare stomach was flat, with little droplets of water…

He spun Helia around in order to regain control over himself.

Swallowing thickly, he lowered his voice just a little as he placed his hands on her arms. 'We're just going to get you used to a simple movement.'

He felt her shudder but pushed on, moving her arms in slow circles.

'I'm no expert, but shouldn't I be doing this *in* the water,' she teased.

'You could try, but I don't think you would enjoy being underwater all that much. I hear breathing is difficult.'

'Fair enough.'

How was it that she made him smile, laugh so easily, when that was the last thing he wanted to do. Why did she make him feel lighter?

Vasili made her practise the strokes until he was certain that she was doing them perfectly.

'Now come to the side,' he instructed. 'You're going to hold on to the wall and kick your legs. Don't worry, I will be holding you,' he added, when he could see she was about to protest.

He helped her into position, placing his hands on her stomach under the water, holding her up while she learnt how to kick the right way. He could hear himself giving her directions, but all he could think about was that she was exactly as soft as he'd thought. That he wanted to say screw the swimming lesson so he could hold her against his body and show her what that damn bikini was doing to him.

Slowly he moved her away from the wall so she could get used to the feel of the water.

'Don't panic. I've got you. I'm not letting go.'

He never wanted to, and now he was cursing himself for offering to teach her—because he might not be able to see her beautiful face or her tempting breasts, but he had a constant eyeful of her perfect derriere. Everything about her was perfect. It was driving him mad.

Every time he had her doing a different movement she would clutch onto him as if he was her lifeline, her body rubbing against his. His hands were all over her, and he was going crazy with want. He couldn't think straight any longer. All he wanted to do was press her against the wall and kiss her. Kiss her until she knew nothing but his name. Hear her scream out for him as he pleasured her in every way he knew for as long as possible.

He drew her back to the shallow end, putting a little distance between them. He had to, or he would have no willpower left.

'I think that's enough for one day.'

'Oh. Um…okay.' She frowned.

'It's been hours. I don't think you want to exhaust yourself on the first day.'

Excuses. And flimsy ones at that. He was trying to run from her because she made him let down his guard. She made him feel less alone. And he couldn't give that power to her.

'Vasili…?' he heard Helia say.

Maybe it had been a mistake, marrying her. If he had listened to Andreas and married some princess he didn't care about he wouldn't be tempted like this. Wouldn't be so attracted to her that he was in physical pain. He would have loathed her too much ever to get close.

'Are you okay?'

Helia had started moving closer to him, and all he could do was make his way to the steps.

'Yes, I've just remembered I have some things to take care of. Will you be okay to entertain yourself?'

'Yes, of course.'

He nodded once and then, without another look at his wife, Vasili grabbed his towel and disappeared into the chalet.

CHAPTER EIGHT

HELIA STOOD BEFORE the large mirror in the bedroom, paint-
ing a deep red colour on her lips. She had been told that as
Queen she would need to be ready to be photographed at
any time. Day or night. If she was in public, she was fair
game. And, while she hoped they would have privacy in
this secluded, empty resort, there were still boats out on
the water. Who knew which of those were equipped with
telephoto lenses? Helia couldn't take any chances.

The sun had gone down, but the air was still warm.
Which was a good thing, because the white toga-like dress
she wore offered little protection from the elements.

Vasili had left a note saying they would be dining together. She supposed that to the world they were on honeymoon, and it would be highly unusual if they weren't seen
together.

As Helia walked along the path, she couldn't stop thinking about their time in the pool earlier.

She had been apprehensive about accepting his offer,
but the idea that she could learn to do something she had
always wanted to had been too tempting.

Vasili had been kind and patient. He'd made her feel
at ease despite her anxiety in the water. It had been hours
of him holding her and touching her. Hours of her heart

skipping a beat with every one of those touches. And his voice… It had poured over her like silk.

She had revelled in his attention, despite the fact that she knew she should have kept her distance, and had fought hard to listen to his instructions—before he had pulled back so hard all she could compare it to was a rubber band snapping back after being stretched to its limit.

Spending time with her couldn't have been so abhorrent to him, could it?

Except it could. Her mere existence had been enough for her uncle to toss her away.

Vasili had fled. And she hadn't seen or heard from him since. Well, apart from the invitation to dinner…

Helia followed the long path until she came to a large deck that extended out onto the sand. Upon it was a single, square table with two chairs, laid with a setting for two. A candle sat in the middle with a dancing flame. And there sat Vasili in a white linen shirt, sleeves rolled up, exposing his forearms. His eyes, his hair, seemed so much darker in the muted light.

A dark prince.

No.

A dark king.

She noticed his eyes widen briefly as she stepped into view, but he quickly recovered, moving to pull out her chair, which he helped her onto before joining her at the table.

'Is something wrong?' Helia racked her brain, still trying to figure out her mistake in the pool.

Vasili simply shook his head. 'Nothing.'

She knew that was a lie.

'You look beautiful.'

'Th-thank you,' she stuttered, feeling off balance.

She looked over his shoulder, just able to make out the

water. The sounds of lapping waves formed the soundtrack to their dinner.

'Wine?' he offered.

'Yes, please.'

Helia could see he was stiff, despite trying to put on an air of ease, and there was something off about the way he spoke to her.

'I don't believe you,' she said, taking a sip of the fruity wine.

'About what?' Vasili was busy pouring himself a glass.

'When you say nothing is wrong. We've only been married two days and already I know something is off. Tell me what I've done.'

'Don't worry about it, Helia.'

'How can I not? We're supposed to be honest with each other, remember?'

Helia thought back to the pool. Everything had been fine and then he'd withdrawn. As if a switch had been flipped. She couldn't recall doing anything to upset him, which left only her actual presence. She should have refused him in the first place.

'I remember. And if something was wrong, I would talk to you about it.' He glanced away from her as something caught his attention. 'The food is arriving.'

'Please don't insult my intelligence.'

She leaned back in her chair and plastered a pleasant smile on her face, thanking the servers as they laid a starter between the two of them. It was a honeymoon dinner meant to be shared between a happy newlywed couple. Not two people awkwardly navigating a marriage of convenience.

Marinated olives, dips and sliced wedges of pitta sat between them. Helia could picture other honeymooning couples feeding each other. A meal to bring couples even closer together. A seduction before returning to their room.

As soon as the servers walked away from the table she leaned forward and spoke softly enough that they wouldn't be overheard. 'If you would like, I can go. I can feign some illness…perhaps say I've spent too long in the sun…so no one would be any the wiser.'

His molars locked. 'I don't want that.'

Helia sighed. 'Fine. Then how about this? A thought for a thought. I'm currently thinking that I did something to offend you earlier, and that if we remain together like this people are going to know something is wrong between their king and queen. So I'm going to offer you a solution. I don't want you to feel forced to spend time with me. For image or for any reason whatsoever. I am well aware of what this marriage is supposed to be, given all I have to think about. We have complete privacy here—you've made sure of that. So you should use this time to mourn your brother in peace and I will respect your privacy.'

Vasili hated himself. Had he thought the way he'd left earlier wouldn't be noticed? That Helia wouldn't take his leaving as a reflection on herself? She had done nothing wrong and yet here she still sat with him, so poised, any emotion on lockdown, offering him a kindness.

He had wounded her. For that he should be the one punished. And yet Helia was the one hurting. It was obvious in her words. She told him he wouldn't have to spend time with her as if that was something to suffer through. Despite whatever negative feelings he had her experiencing, she still considered *his* feelings. His grief. When had anyone ever done that?

She had known him only a few days, but had already

shown him a support he hadn't experienced. He hadn't known it could feel like this. As if there was an immovable wall at his back. Someone to say, *I've got you.*

But he couldn't accept the offer. Tempting as it was. He wouldn't mourn when it was convenient. He wouldn't ask for help. The void that had been torn into him when he'd been told his brother was dead only yawned wider, but he would deal with his grief just as he had dealt with everything else in his life. Alone.

And just like that the safety of that wall disintegrated and he was alone, fighting through the world on his own again.

'That won't be necessary, Helia.'

He reached over, picking up a piece of pitta to give his hands something to do, somewhere safe to focus, and spread dip along the bread. He noticed that apart from her sip of wine Helia reached for nothing else. Once the bread was loaded to his satisfaction he placed it on her plate, wishing he could pull her onto his lap and feed her instead.

'Vasili…'

Was that exasperation in her tone?

'Helia…?' he mimicked, and chuckled at the unimpressed look on her face. 'I am sorry for the way I left earlier, but I don't need time to mourn.'

'Of course you do. Everyone does.'

'"Everyone" doesn't have the same responsibilities I do,' he replied as he took a bite of his own bread, happy to see Helia had done the same.

'No, they don't, but that doesn't mean you have to ignore your needs. You don't have to deal with everything alone, you know.'

If she only knew. 'I'm not alone. I'm with a beautiful woman.'

'You're changing the subject.'

She plucked an olive from the bowl, and his body stirred to life as he watched her bring it to her lips and close her eyes as she savoured the taste. But then she blinked, tilting her head to the side. Something he'd noticed she did whenever she was trying to understand him.

'Why is that?' she asked.

'I'm *not* changing the subject.'

'And now you're lying. You have a tell. Did you know that?'

'What?'

'You blink and look away,' Helia said matter-of-factly.

'It seems to me you have far too much time on your hands if you've been studying me so closely.'

'And now you're deflecting.' She smirked.

This woman. She was driving him crazy.

'Fine, we'll talk about something else,' she said. 'You've been here before?'

The change of topic seemed safe, but Vasili had the distinct impression that he was not the one on higher ground in this conversation.

'I have.'

'I imagine the parties here would be rather spectacular.'

She was fishing, and the realisation had a smile curving his lips. 'I wouldn't know.'

'You wouldn't?' She frowned.

'I wouldn't, because I have only ever come here alone.'

She constantly made him feel as if he was standing on quicksand—well, now he saw an opportunity to flip the tables on her.

'This is where I come when I need some privacy. A bit of peace and quiet away from everyone.'

She was about to take a bite, but placed her food back down. 'But you've brought me here. Why would you do that?'

Vasili reached over and picked an olive off her plate, popping it into his mouth. 'Why, indeed.'

'I don't always understand you,' she confessed softly.

'Well, then, maybe you need to study harder.'

The idea that someone would know him was enticing—because no one had ever bothered to. The only person who had was taken from him when he was a teenager and all those who were left would never see the value in his existence. Vasili had never invested his time in relationships because they were fleeting anyway, but he knew that he risked becoming a cold ruler who thought only of the Kingdom and not of his wife.

Wouldn't he then become the very thing he didn't want to be? Just like his parents? Of course he would. But want wasn't need, and he needed to ensure that he never let Helia behind his walls. If only she'd agreed to his terms they would have something else to focus on, and he could distract her in ways that kept him safe.

That night, when they climbed into bed and Vasili turned down the lights, he was prepared for his body's response to his wife.

Preparation didn't make it any easier to bear.

'Vasili?' Her voice cut through the darkness.

'Hmm?'

'Can I ask you something?'

'Anything.'

'Why do you hate it so much?'

'Hate what?'

'The throne. The title. Everything.'

He trained his eyes on a spot in the distance. With all the doors and windows open, he could see a sliver of moonlight cast across the craggy cliffs. He didn't know how much to reveal, so he opted for the shortest, safest answer.

'It's a cage.'

It caged one's heart, so one could never show real love to those who deserved to receive it. Caged one's spirit, so one would always be what the institution expected. Caged one's soul, so one would never have true freedom.

He knew Helia would be reading something into the silence that followed. She was perceptive. Intelligent. She would know there was so much he wasn't saying.

'I know I haven't agreed to your terms yet, and that we may never have a traditional marriage and I won't expect one. But maybe we could be friends.'

He could tell she was waiting for him to respond, and when he didn't, she went on.

'I just think we could both use a friend on this journey, or it could be a very long, very unhappy life. And I don't think either of us deserves that.'

Still, he couldn't respond.

She let out a sigh and turned over so her back was to him. 'Just think about it. Goodnight, Vasili.'

He lay there in the dark night, listening to the ocean and replaying her words in his head. Finally, he heard her breath even out, and once she was soundly asleep he said, 'I don't know how to be a friend, Helia. All I know is how to be alone.'

CHAPTER NINE

THAT NIGHT VASILI lay awake for hours, and when he did fall asleep it wasn't very long before he woke. He found Helia in his arms, but instead of extricating himself from the tangle of their sleepy embrace he pulled her more tightly to him. Breathing in her scent. Pondering the fact that even in sleep their attraction had them gravitating towards each other.

It was exactly what he had been afraid of. And even more worrying was how much he wanted to keep holding on to her. He couldn't need her like this. He wouldn't allow himself to.

She was right, he had to concede. It would be an unbearably long life spent in misery if they continued as they were now. He was only twenty-nine, she barely a year younger. They had their whole lives ahead of them. The issue was that Vasili had spent most of his life alone. There were always people around him, and yet there was never a person *with* him.

If he didn't have friends, how could he be one?

He wouldn't consider himself an adequate one for Helia, that was for certain. She was a good person. Didn't she deserve a better friend than he could be?

Even as he thought that he knew he couldn't stay away entirely. He wanted to explore her body. To know her. So, while he might not have the ability to be a friend, or a husband, or even a good king, he could make an effort for Helia while maintaining his boundaries. He would endure this attraction until she gave him her promise that she would accept a life on his terms.

Which meant he would have to start spending time with her and not fleeing as he had done the day before.

Vasili eased away from Helia and slipped a shirt over his head. He called room service for coffee while thinking about how he could spend the day with Helia while remaining cordial and pleasant, and then he made another call.

He settled on the edge of the bed. 'Helia,' he said gently. She scrunched up her nose, letting out an irritated grunt that made his heart twinge. 'I have a surprise waiting. I think you'd be most displeased if you missed out on it because you'd slept all day.'

'It's not all day,' she mumbled.

She tried to turn away from him, and Vasili could see the exact moment that her brain caught up with the rest of her. Eyes widening, she moved to sit up.

'Vasili, I'm—'

'Come on, there's coffee waiting and you need to get ready.'

'Why are we awake so early?'

Helia ran her fingers through her hair, bunching it over her shoulder. Vasili followed the movement, picturing his fingers tangled in her locks.

'You are a prickly one in the morning—do you know that?'

She only looked at him, with no expression on her face.

He felt his lips twitch into a smile. 'The surprise is out on the water.'

'Great. So it's not for me.'

'Oh, no, you don't.' He grabbed the covers as she tried sinking further down into the bed. 'I expect you outside in fifteen minutes.'

With a glare and a few mumbled words she tossed the covers off. 'I'm up.'

It didn't take her long to get dressed, and when she emerged in yet another mind-boggling bikini, with a sheer dress over it, Vasili knew it would be a very long day.

'I didn't think kings were meant to wear shorts,' she teased, taking in his outfit.

'They do when they're on honeymoon at the beach.'

'So where are we going?' Helia asked as she fell into step beside him.

'You'll see.'

He led her along various paths, all of which he had explored on his own over the years, until they came to a pier with a single boat docked. Polished wood and shiny fibreglass gleamed in the morning sun.

'Vasili, I can't...'

'I won't let anything happen to you, Helia.'

He'd anticipated that she would be nervous, and waited for her to give him a sign that she was ready to go aboard. Eventually she gave him a small nod, and he climbed aboard the luxury runabout then helped her in.

He felt a tremor running through her as the vessel bucked and swayed. Her eyes darted to each end of the boat and out to sea. She was nervous. That much was obvious. And with her not being able to swim he wasn't surprised. But he'd meant what he said. He would never let any harm befall her.

Vasili picked up a bright red lifejacket and brought it around her, guiding her arms through the sleeves, his eyes locked on hers as he did up the clasps on the front, his breathing turning heavy as goosebumps erupted on her skin. Gently pushing her arms out, Vasili found himself once again tightly strapping Helia up. Her body obeyed his silent commands so easily. She was so soft…so delicate. He had to concentrate to ignore the desire coursing through him from having Helia beneath his hands.

'Sit here.' He helped her into one of the four seats in the open boat. 'Nothing bad is going to happen, but you can hold on to this handle if you need to,' he said, his voice growing gruff as he placed her hand on one of the grip handles. 'Even if you end up in the water, don't panic. Your jacket will keep you buoyant and I will get you. Do you understand?'

'Yes.'

'Good.'

He wanted to lean down and kiss her, but he would not touch her yet, and wrenched himself away to the steering wheel. He refused to look at Helia. Instead, he eased the boat away from the pier and out to open waters.

'Where are we going?' she asked.

'Somewhere special,' he answered.

They were already somewhere special. Choosing to honeymoon at this resort had been for his own benefit as well as hers. Everything they would do after they went back to Seidon would be for public consumption, so a little break with some privacy was a small comfort he could offer Helia. Why he was taking her to another special place was beyond him. And he wasn't going to examine it.

They left the resort far behind as they approached a small island in the archipelago. Slowing the boat down, he brought it to a halt at a tiny uninhabited island. He grabbed a basket from the rear seat—judging from her confused frown, Helia hadn't noticed it. He wasn't surprised. She'd been nervous on the entire boat ride, holding on to the handle in a white-knuckled grip.

They made their way onto the beach—Vasili's favourite place in the whole of Thalonia. People didn't usually come out to this island, so apart from the sound of the water and the gulls flying above there was utter stillness. Even the sounds of the water seemed far away.

'It's beautiful here.'

He glanced over at Helia, who had her arms wrapped around herself, staring out over the calm water. The breeze was blowing her hair out to the side.

'It is,' he said, putting the basket down and moving behind her. He lowered his head so his lips were at her ear and pointed over the water. 'See those cliffs on either side?' He felt Helia nod. 'They keep the waves out, so the water here is always calm.'

It was true. There was just a gentle lapping on the shore. All the beautiful violence of the waves was contained in the distance.

'It's safe for you to get into the water here. With me, of course,' he added.

'This is a wonderful surprise. Thank you for bringing me here. Even if you drove the boat too fast.' She stared accusingly at him as he stepped away.

'You'll get used to it.'

Would she? Did he plan on bringing her back here? Vasili hadn't consciously thought about it, but he felt centred here. As if he could be anyone. With a million choices before him. It was likely that Helia would need a break too, over the years to come, so why wouldn't they return?

That answer was a cloud hanging over them... What if her answer to his rules was no?

'What's that?'

She broke through his musings, tipping her chin towards the basket.

'I'd hope a librarian would know.'

Helia rewarded him with an eye-roll.

'I've had a picnic prepared for us. The question is, do you want to swim before or after?'

'Before. I'm already nervous as it is. I don't need to eat before getting in the water.'

'You'll be fine, Helia. Swim it is.'

Vasili pulled his shirt over his head, depositing it on the sand, and watched Helia shedding her dress to reveal a bright blue swimsuit. His hands curled into fists as he attempted to smother the urges running rampant through him.

With her hand in his, they waded out into the water, and when they were chest-deep he stopped and allowed her to get used to the push and pull of the current.

'Please don't let go,' she begged.

'I won't. You can trust me.'

'I do.'

Vasili wanted to warn her that she shouldn't, but he couldn't deny that it satisfied some deep need in him to hear someone say it.

'I used to watch the crowds back home playing in the water and wish I could join them. It's funny…something as simple as frolicking at the beach can mean so much.'

Helia looked around the cove, seeing nothing but nature. Vasili had not only given her a taste of something she had always wanted, but he'd made sure to do it somewhere she would be safe and away from prying eyes.

'Why are you being so kind to me?'

His grip on her loosened. 'Would you rather I did not

care about your well-being? I thought you wanted a friend in this marriage?'

'I do, but after you've been forced to be King and to marry me, I don't understand why you would do something like this for me.'

Helia knew he was kind. She had seen it in his interactions around the palace. But now that his kindness was directed at her, it was hard not to feel something for Vasili—and this was exactly why she hadn't yet agreed to his terms.

'I was forced to marry, Helia. I wasn't forced to marry you. I made that choice.'

She noticed a frown flash across his face. There and gone.

'You weren't given much choice either, and that is my fault. This is the least I can do. I wish I knew your reasons for agreeing…maybe one day you will be comfortable enough to tell me.'

'Maybe.'

'I know so little of you.'

'What do you want to know?'

'Anything. Tell me about a good memory.'

That wasn't what she had expected. She'd thought he would ask all the standard questions people asked when they attempted to get to know someone. Not Vasili. He wanted to know her heart. And maybe she could understand that, since he would have had to question the motives of every person in his life.

Helia wasn't accustomed to sharing parts of herself with others, but for some reason she knew her most treasured memory would be safe with him.

'My father was a florist, and every evening he would return home with a flower for me from the shop. Just one.

I had a vase in my room, and by the end of every week it would hold a bouquet of beautiful mismatched flowers. I loved it.'

'Which were your favourite?' Vasili asked.

He seemed genuinely interested in her answer, and it allowed her to lose herself in the memory. It was as if she didn't have to have her guard up, protecting her precious memories.

'The irises. There were so many colours.' Helia looked away, a small huff of laughter passing through her lips.

'What?'

'It's just that I've never told anyone about that before.'

Maybe that was because she was too afraid to form friendships, lest those friends abandoned her too.

Hope had lived in the halls of the orphanage. A blessing and a curse. There had always been the hope that someone would be chosen by a family and would leave. It had rarely happened. And even if it had the rest of them would soon be alone again. If you were old enough to hope, you were usually too old to be adopted.

Vasili's hand went around her waist, while the other cupped her cheek. There was nothing but utter sincerity in his eyes. 'I'm honoured that you would tell me.'

It scared Helia that when it came to Vasili she was hopeful again. That was why she'd told him such a personal memory. She knew he couldn't leave, given the reason they had married, but was it smart to open herself up to him when he wouldn't ever be there for her emotionally?

It was then she noticed that while she had been distracted he had taken her further out, and she had been treading water just as he had been. As if her body naturally followed his lead.

What would it be like to dance with him?

She wondered where that thought had come from. She had never danced in her life.

'I can't believe I'm doing this,' she said, incredulous.

A pulsing rhythm beat between them. The air was growing taut. Could Vasili feel it too?

'You're a fast learner, but I'd rather not push you. Shall we go back to shore and see what's in the picnic basket?'

He was forcing her away, but she knew then that he was just as affected. 'I'd like that.'

After drying themselves off, and keeping a respectable distance from each other, Vasili pulled two flute glasses and a bottle of champagne from the basket, followed by strawberries, dips, and an assortment of finger foods. The resort kitchen had gone all out.

Helia picked up a particularly deep red strawberry. Vasili's eyes darkened and she saw him track the path of the fruit to her lips and the bite she took. Sweet flavour exploded on her tongue. Juice dripped down her hand, and she quickly licked it away.

It looked as if he was grinding his teeth.

'So, I told you a memory—now it's your turn.'

He cleared his throat, and his voice seemed a touch lower. 'What do you want to know?'

'The same. A good memory.'

She could see him thinking. Taking a long time to do so.

'Is it really that hard to think of one?'

'Yes.' But before she could comment further, he was talking. 'When Leander and I were children he would sneak into my room at night. At first he used to steal treats from the kitchens and bring them up, but I got better at it than him. I would smuggle our contraband into my room and every night we would spend a few hours gorging on snacks.'

'You were close?'

'Not especially. He had a destiny he had to be prepared for. It didn't leave us a lot of time for bonding.'

Helia didn't want to point out that from where she sat it seemed they'd been incredibly close. What she wouldn't have given to have had a sibling all those years in the orphanage. She also got the distinct impression that Vasili wasn't telling her the full truth. That was okay. She would just listen to what he felt safe revealing. Maybe one day he would share more.

'You miss him a lot, don't you?' she said.

'I do. Champagne?'

'Yes, please.'

She allowed him to change the topic.

'You said you hadn't flown before, but have you travelled anywhere?'

'A few times we went on holiday to a cabin in the forest a few hours outside of Seidon. It was beautiful there. Peaceful. Just my father and I.'

'May I ask how he passed away?'

She was aware of how closely Vasili watched her. 'An aneurysm.'

Like a switch, her whole life had changed after that.

'I'm sorry.'

He reached over and took her hand in his. Over the years, Helia had grown numb to the sympathy she would receive when anyone found out she was an orphan, but with Vasili she wanted to lean into him. It felt as if he was offering comfort and warmth. It was that dangerous hope again—but this man had shown her there was a depth to him that not many chose to see, so Helia believed his kindness.

'Thank you. Can I make a confession?' she asked.

'Should I be concerned?'

'No.' She laughed. 'I saw you the first day I started working at the palace.'

'You did?' He sat up straighter, enticed by this titbit of information.

'You were wearing black leathers and climbing on to your motorcycle. I thought you were rather sexy. Unusual, but sexy.' She could feel herself blush.

'You did, did you?' He smirked.

'I also thought your ego probably didn't need inflating.'

'Lie.'

'What?'

'That was a lie, Helia. I'll let it go this time. If you like, I could take you on a ride.'

'A king out on a motorbike?' she scoffed.

'Why not? Who's going to stop me?'

Helia held her glass between both hands as she leaned towards the King. 'You know, you say you don't want to be King, but you seem to have taken to it just fine.'

Vasili shrugged.

'Also, there is no way I'm getting on that death machine.'

'Scared?' he taunted.

'Yes! I can't even drive a car, and that has four wheels. You're out of your mind if you think I'm getting on two.'

'You can't drive?'

Helia shook her head. Another thing she'd never had the opportunity to learn. A fairly basic skill at that.

'Well, then, we'll just have to teach you how.'

Helia laughed, even though the idea appealed to her more than it should. 'I'm not sure we'll have the time.'

'I'll make the time.'

'I know I've said it before, but thank you for bringing me here, Vasili. It's the most relaxed I've been in a long time. You know, I never dreamed of anything like this. A life like the one I'm living now. It feels like I've stepped through a portal into an alternative reality and I'm struggling to wrap my head around it.'

'You can ask for help, Helia.'

Just like her, he kept his gaze over the sea, and she was grateful for that because it made it easier to be honest with him.

'From whom? Andreas? Carissa?'

'Me?' he replied.

Helia shook her head. Of course he would offer. He was ensuring his queen would be competent, and the woman in the palace office before they'd left was not.

'I'm sorry for failing with Andreas. I don't know how to wield this power I have just yet. I'm so afraid of doing or saying the wrong thing.'

'You'll learn, Helia. I don't expect you to handle this world with the level of mastery that only comes with years of experience. And there was no harm done. I was there to support you as I said I would be.'

'But what if you weren't?' Helia challenged.

'That won't happen. I got you into this—I'm not going to abandon you to the sharks now.' Vasili abruptly stood and turned to her. 'I'm going back in the water.'

Helia moved through the shallows to perch on a rock. She watched him keenly as he waded out into the sea. The muscles on his back rippled as he dived in. She bit down on her lip, appreciating the way the water glided over his body as he surged through it in powerful strokes. That was her husband. A man she had admired. And as she peeled back the layers of him, she found there was so much more to him.

Helia was coming to realise that she was growing fond of him—which meant that she couldn't accept his terms. They hadn't shared in any pleasure yet, and she was already developing some sort of feeling for him. Not to mention the fact that she still didn't know where she stood when it came to children, which meant that wasn't a firm no, as Vasili wanted.

That didn't stop her watching him swim until he was a speck in the distance, and she didn't take her eyes off him until he was walking towards her. Beads of water raced down his sculpted body, raining down from his hair. He was a masterpiece, and maybe her lust for him was evident on her face because his gaze was fixed on her too. Devouring her.

They might have been outdoors, but the air had become thick. Charged like it had been at the church when they'd kissed.

The force of his presence tugged her off the rock and, paying little attention to her movements, she slipped. But there was no splash of her falling into the water as she'd expected to. Instead, strong hands caught her, and when she looked up golden-brown eyes were all she saw.

She couldn't stop herself then, but neither could Vasili, and their lips crashed together, stealing the breath from her. Making her heart pound and liquid heat pool in her core. Then his tongue caressed hers and she shivered against him. His arms tightened around her, making her forget where she stood or why she was there. Forget all that she had decided moments before.

His lips slid against hers, tasting of the salty sea. Her skin heated. His touches were making her light-headed. She was reminded how explosive they were together. This could be hers to experience for all her life...

Helia really didn't want to step out of Vasili's embrace.

So what if they wouldn't have children? She didn't have them now, didn't have any family, so it wouldn't change anything. And even if he couldn't be there for her emotion-ally, she hadn't ever needed anyone to be. She had survived and made it this far on her own. But their chemistry…? This was new. This was exciting. And she wanted much more of it, so maybe it would be enough.

'Vasili…' His name caught in a breath. He hummed low in his throat, igniting a spark in her belly. 'I agree to your terms.'

CHAPTER TEN

'SAY THAT AGAIN,' he'd breathed against her lips.

'I agree to your terms, Vasili, all of them.'

It had been as if her words had unleashed the tidal wave of want he had been trying to control, and he'd kissed her. He'd kissed her as he'd carried her out of the water, and he'd kept on kissing her until the sun had travelled across the sky and they'd had to return to the resort.

Now they sat on the deck once more beneath the night sky—still in their beachwear, having not bothered to return to the chalet—after enjoying yet another dinner. This one had been far more pleasant than the previous one.

'Take a walk with me.'

He had meant it to be a question, but it hadn't come out that way. Not when he wanted so much to extend their day.

'Of course.'

It should have worried him that Helia was so ready to spend more time with him, but he couldn't care now. He took her hand in his, leading her away from the deck and onto the sand, where they kept walking until they reached a dark beach the lights of the resort could not reach. The moon was reflected on the water, giving only just enough silvery light to see where they were going.

'What are we doing here?' Helia asked.

'You'll see. This should be fine.' He sat on the sand, pulling her down with him. 'Lie back.'

He let go of her hand and folded his arms behind his head, pleased when she followed suit.

The black sky was covered in silvery twinkling stars. The Milky Way was like an airbrushed stripe across the sky in blues, purples and blacks.

'It's breathtaking!' Helia exclaimed.

'It is. The lights in Seidon are too bright to see the stars, so whenever I come out here I take a moment to appreciate them. The quiet…'

'It's so peaceful. Thank you for sharing this with me.'

He wanted to thank her for being there with him. Even if she hadn't agreed to his rules it would have been a good day. Probably the best Vasili had experienced in a very long time. Maybe ever. He didn't want it to end—which was probably rather selfish of him. Helia was likely tired. He knew he should let her retire for the night. But he couldn't let her go. And yet he couldn't ask her to stay. He had never asked for anything in life. He moved through it alone. Did things for himself. He didn't need people, so the words would not form.

The sand beside him shifted. Helia had moved closer. As if she could sense the need in him. He couldn't stop himself. He unfurled one arm, placing it under her, scooping her closer to his body.

'You know, according to myth, Hera created the Milky Way.'

Helia placed her palm on his chest. The warmth seared him to his core.

'Heracles needed that strength for his labours.' He took great pride in the look of surprise on Helia's face. 'What? Do you think princes don't read?'

'It's not that. I just wouldn't have expected you to be allowed to read about mythology when you must have had a prescribed book list.'

'I could read whatever I wanted to. Why would you think otherwise?'

'I've been given a list of what *I* should read.'

'You can read whatever you want, Helia. You're the Queen. As someone once said, "Make it so."'

'Just like that?'

'Just like that.'

Vasili brushed his fingers through her hair. Now that Helia had agreed, and he had permitted himself to touch her, he couldn't stop. He hated it. And he loved it.

'There may be things you need to read to prepare you for ruling, but you're not limited to what Andreas thinks is appropriate. He's pining for the kind of rulers he's never going to get.'

'What about you?'

That was a loaded question. What did Vasili want? Initially he had been opposed to being King, but now he had accepted the title. He was King; and when he thought about who should rule beside him he could think of no better option than her. Which had him answering honestly.

'I'm happy with the Queen I have.'

He didn't wait for her to respond. Couldn't bear to see what reaction she might have. So he pulled away and stood up, ripping his shirt over his head and offering her his hand.

'Take a swim with me.'

'Now?'

'Yes.'

'But…'

'Don't be afraid, Helia. Trust me.'

He wanted her to, and when Helia put her hand in his

it was easy to ignore that voice at the back of his mind screaming at him to get away from her. Warning him that he was getting too close. He wanted to listen to it, but at the same time he craved that closeness with equal measure.

Vasili took her into the water. His hands tight around hers.

'Please don't let go of me.'

'I won't.'

When they were waist-deep, he turned to look at her. He had thought at the cove that she looked like some sort of sea nymph, with those eyes the colour of the water, her golden body and the blue bikini, but now... Now she looked ethereal. Utterly ravishing in the pale moonlight. Who cared about Hera or the Milky Way when he had a goddess in his arms? Except she wasn't...not yet.

He let go of her hand to wrap his arms around her waist, holding her close. Her sharp intake of breath raised the hairs on his body. He wanted to make her gasp. He wanted to make her as crazy as she made him.

Eyes locked on hers, he leaned in...waiting. Praying that she would close the distance between them. Making sure that she was certain it was her choice. He would let her go if she didn't. Let her go back to the bedroom and give her enough time to fall asleep before he went anywhere near the place and faced another night of little to no sleep. Of craving Helia like air and avoiding even the barest hint of intimacy.

But he wouldn't have to. While he knew he would still have to face his battles, Vasili rejoiced as she closed the gap between their lips. Pressing hers against his in a desperate bid to get closer. He angled his head and she parted her lips for him. His fingers were digging into the soft skin at her waist as their tongues met in a sweet dance. She clutched at his back, wanting more. And he would give it.

He deepened the kiss, growing hard at the sound of her moan. She would feel his length pressed up against her, he knew it, but he couldn't step away. He wanted her so badly it was a buzzing throughout his body.

'Helia…' he breathed against her lips.

Was he asking her permission to go further? Was he trying to stop? He didn't know.

He pulled away slightly and her soft fingers came up to his lips. Tracing the outline of them. Need was singing through his blood.

'Is this real?' she whispered.

'Yes.'

It was all he could manage before his hand was at the back of her head and he was kissing her again. Harder. Deeper. Nipping at her lip as desire flooded his body. Her hands were sliding down his chest, making his breath catch, but they stopped on his stomach and he almost begged her to keep going. He trailed his lips along his jaw, to her ear. He understood her question…it seemed like a dream to him too.

'I need to touch you. Please,' he begged.

'Yes.'

One little word that nearly undid him.

With one arm firmly around her, he slid his other hand down her neck, over her chest, cupping her breast. She mewled against him as he rubbed his thumb over her nipple, so he did it again.

'I need more,' she begged him.

'Tell me what you want,' he said against her neck.

'Vasili, please…'

'Tell me how to serve you, Helia.'

'Touch me…there.'

He trailed his lips over her neck and cheek and just as slowly trailed his fingers down her stomach, dipping below the water and under the waistband of her panties. She shuddered against him. Moaned as his lips closed over hers at the same time as his fingers slipped into her core, finding her slick for him.

He stroked her until she was panting. Every sound she made was driving him into a frenzy of lust. He was painfully hard now, but all he cared about was Helia's pleasure. He needed her release as if it was his own. It was a new feeling to him. Pleasure was always mutual, and then it was over, but here in the water with Helia he never wanted it to end.

Helia could barely think. His kisses were stoking the flame of her desire while his fingers pushed her further and further to the edge. But she was afraid of the fall. It felt so good here. She didn't want to think of what came after. So she tried with all her might to hold on to this feeling. This blazing heat consuming her. The water was doing nothing to extinguish the flames. If anything, the constant gentle waves were adding to her pleasure.

Her fingers slid down Vasili's body, gripping the waistband of his shorts. She felt him tense. Felt the twitch of his hardness against her body. She wanted to touch him.

Helia had fantasised about this. Being in his arms. To give and receive pleasure. Her fantasies had been positively dull compared to what she felt now. Her rough breaths grew ever more rapid. There was a coiling in her belly. She wanted him to feel it too.

'You feel like heaven, Helia,' Vasili said, kissing his way down her throat.

'I want to touch you too.'

'Not yet.'

'Why not?'

'Because right now I need you to come apart for me. And when you do touch me I want to be able to see you... and for you to see a king fall apart at your touch.'

Helia was barely hanging on, his words sending a shock of arousal through her. And as if Vasili could tell just how close she was, he slipped a finger into her, then another. He was curling them and making them hit a spot that had her seeing stars far brighter than the ones overhead.

'Vasili!' she cried out as she shattered around his fingers.

He pulled her against him even tighter, kissing her hungrily, stroking her and drawing out her pleasure until she felt weak-kneed.

And then she was in his arms and they were moving out of the water, Vasili carrying her to their chalet.

He took them straight into the large shower, where they washed off the sea and sand. Vasili made her come apart on his fingers again, and all the while he wouldn't let her return the favour, making her grow tense. Self-conscious. Maybe he'd had a taste of their passion and found her lacking. Her experience was limited, after all.

She climbed into the bed and he slid in after her, propping his head up on his hand. Lying on her back, she looked into his eyes, and could see swirling thoughts behind them. In the light of the room she could see the haze of lust dissipate, gone from his features to be replaced by something else.

She prayed it wasn't regret.

'Just say it, Vasili.'

He put an arm over her, holding her tightly against him. 'I don't yet fully understand your reasons for choosing to marry me, Helia, but I can only imagine a marriage like this isn't something you envisaged for yourself.'

Marriage was something Helia had only thought of as a concept—not as something she would ever truly experience. Not when she was so afraid of being abandoned. Trust didn't come easily, and it was far safer to be on her own because she knew she could rely on herself. It was a huge part of why her only relationship had failed.

She tried to respond to Vasili, but he silenced her.

'Let me finish. I want you. Probably more than you can comprehend...'

Helia had an idea, but she wouldn't tell him how she felt about him and for quite how long she had felt that way.

'Tonight...what transpired between us...it's only the tip of the iceberg. And I was honest with you. I do want you to touch me. I do want you to give me pleasure in the way I have given it to you. But I need to be sure you understand and have fully considered our terms. I can't love you, Helia. I'm not capable of that. We won't ever be husband and wife in the traditional sense. And I am sorry about that, but it's just the way it is.'

All Helia had done since their talk was consider his terms, but her heart still broke at hearing the words. She'd always known she wouldn't be enough for him. Being just an ordinary woman from Seidon. They were worlds apart, and his words struck right at those insecurities. But she was also hurt at him saying he wasn't capable of love, because the very fact that he was grieving for Leander meant that he was.

Maybe his problem wasn't that he wasn't capable of love but rather that he loved too much—not that it would mean much for her. He had just admitted that he couldn't ever love her.

'I have already agreed, Vasili.' She hoped her voice would not betray the hurt she was trying to hide from him. 'I remember we are united in our duty as King and Queen to the world's eyes, and that in our home we explore this attraction between us. But no sex. No love. No children.'

She waved between their bodies.

'This is the only way I can give myself to you, Helia,' he said. 'And if you have any apprehension at all, then I think it's best if we don't cross that boundary.'

'I thought you weren't interested in me? You said you shouldn't have kissed me.'

'Nothing could be further from the truth. I have made my attraction to you plain. I meant that I shouldn't have kissed you like I did at the wedding, but I had wanted to since you walked into my office.'

Helia hadn't realised that she could feel two such conflicting emotions at the same time. It hurt to know that no matter how long they would spend together she would never have his love, but she did want to be with him. And to find out that he was so attracted to her had made the unbroken parts of her heart soar.

However, a lifetime was a very long passage. To travel the entirety of it without love would be difficult. Would their chemistry last? Was it a good enough substitute? Could a physical relationship ever be enough?

If she didn't accept these terms then she would have no relationship with him at all. Perhaps a cordial friendship, with time. And that seemed like a path filled with misery. Not to mention the fact that her goals depended on her remaining as Queen. So she really only had one choice. Because she did want to be with him, and having some of him was a much better prospect than having none of him.

'I can do this.'

She placed her hand on his cheek and he leaned into her palm. Right then, despite the fractures forming through her, she knew she made the correct choice.

'I want this.'

He kissed her palm and then her lips in a slow, lingering caress. 'That makes me happy.'

She ran her fingers through his soft hair, saw his golden-brown eyes alight with heat. 'Me too.'

But she was feeling nowhere near as euphoric as she'd thought she would.

'I'm going to show you so much pleasure,' he whispered in her ear.

And she let the intoxication of his embrace carry her away from the heaviness in her heart.

CHAPTER ELEVEN

VASILI OPENED HIS EYES. It took him a few moments to remember he was back in the palace, sleeping in the King's bed. Gone were all his books and his tranquil walls. Instead, his senses were assaulted by a gaudy room and an ornate four-poster bed.

Also behind him was his honeymoon.

The remaining days had passed far too quickly, with Vasili exploring Helia's body for as long and as frequently as he'd been able to. He had taken great pride in making her scream out his name or having her forget what she was saying with a single look from him.

He was happy that Helia had fully accepted the terms of their relationship, and having an outlet for their attraction made it easier to be in her company—especially since he could barely keep his hands off her. It was a shield between him and Helia while they safely explored their physical connection without any risk of growing attached. But still, every kiss, every taste of her drew him in. So he knew sex was still too big a risk. That kind of intimacy with Helia would be different from anything he had before, and he had to protect himself.

He heaved a sigh. This would take a great deal of getting used to.

What made it all the more unbearable was the fact that his wife was asleep in his arms. A more perfect sight he couldn't imagine, and it was the reason he had struggled through yet another night without much sleep.

The nights, he found, were the hardest.

In his previous life Vasili hadn't minded sleeping next to his conquests, because he'd known they would be gone as soon as the sun was up and he would have little or nothing to do with them again. With Helia it was much, much different. She was meant to be his partner, and he was growing fond of her, but sleeping in the same bed as her for the sake of appearances without the excuse of sex still felt far too intimate. As if he was inviting her into his heart for her company. For her heart. To create a bond.

He couldn't have that.

Not when all he'd experienced was being cast aside when he'd craved a bond with his family. When he'd been young and naïve and had trusted that they would be there for him and love him even if they were busy. It had never happened, and it had taught him a lesson to keep his heart walled off. To forsake the bonds that people usually sought.

So he couldn't lower his guard, which meant he never relaxed enough to rest, and therefore was continuously tormented by her presence in the dark.

'Helia,' he called gently as he pulled away from her. 'We have an appearance to make.'

As he had been instructed, Andreas had ensured that the orphanage was ready for their visit.

She groaned, burrowing deeper into her pillow. Vasili curled his hands into fists, fighting the urge to brush her hair away from her face.

'You don't want to keep the children waiting.'

'No.' She yawned, stretching her body, and Vasili

couldn't help himself. He pulled her under him, kissing the strip of her exposed stomach. Kissing a path up her torso until his lips locked with hers.

'A girl could get used to this sort of wake-up.'

'A queen,' he said, low-voiced in her ear. 'And you'd better get out of this bed before I keep us both here indefinitely.'

It was so much easier to fall into passion. To ease the ache of want with physicality that still allowed him his barriers.

'Don't threaten me with a good time, Vasili.' She grinned.

'Are you ready for today?'

It was one thing for her to be a queen within the palace walls, quite another to be one in public.

'I think I am. Andreas went over the itinerary and what is expected of me. I think I'm prepared.'

'There will be media.'

He could see her tense. The apprehension in her face.

'I'm sure I'll manage.'

'You don't have to manage, Helia. If it becomes too much, lean on me. Understood?'

He was far more experienced at dealing with all the attention, and truthfully still felt a twinge of guilt for having brought Helia into this mess. The least he could do was make it easier on her. Vasili was aware that there was still a chance that this life could turn him into someone like his parents, so he would choose to be different—and being considerate of his wife was one of those choices.

'Yes,' she said.

She placed her hand on his cheek, and he felt his body responding to the warm touch. If he didn't leave the bed now, he wasn't going to.

* * *

Vasili waited in the palace hall dressed in a blue suit. Everything had been picked out for him. Every piece considered for the image the palace wanted to present. He could only imagine what Helia would be put through this morning. He hoped Andreas and Carissa were going easy on her. It ground on his nerves, the way they treated her, and he would very soon be having a conversation with both of them.

Thankfully, he wasn't allowed to stew for very long as Helia descended the grand staircase, looking an absolute vision. Her hair had been left curly and loose, pulled back, away from her face. Her make-up had been done softly enough that the woman he'd been on honeymoon with was still clearly on display. And that dress… White satin flowed over her body to her narrow waist, where it flared out in pale blue and green flowers to her calves. He wanted to run his hands all over her. Place them on that narrow waist and whisk her away somewhere they could be alone.

'Beautiful,' he said.

'You don't look too bad yourself, Your Majesty.'

He could see the way she looked at him. As if she would like nothing more than to rip away his suit. In just a few days, Helia had gone from being shy and inhibited, unsure if she should touch him, to demanding. Almost confident in her want for pleasure. It satisfied him greatly that she would share that side of herself with him.

Vasili took her hand in his. They would no doubt be photographed from the moment they stepped out of the palace. Together they climbed into the waiting Rolls-Royce bearing the flags of Thalonia.

The ride to the orphanage was longer than he'd thought it would be. Upmarket buildings faded into modest storefronts, which morphed into more battered structures. Seidon had always been the pride of the Kingdom. Its streets were supposed to be rich. His parents would have had everyone believe that the people were happy, but here they looked forgotten. There was none of the vibrancy, none of the life he would have associated with his home. These streets were nothing like the ones he had partied in or ridden his motorcycle along. There wasn't any freedom here.

'Even as a commoner, you don't get choices. You have to make do with what you get dealt.'

Helia's voice came back to him…her words from their first meeting.

Without realising it, he curled his hand tighter around hers and she squeezed back.

They arrived at a nondescript white building. Cameras were already flashing. A line of people waited at the entrance, and once the car door was opened Vasili stepped out, then helped Helia, who emerged with a smile and a wave. It wasn't a bright smile. There was a tightness around her eyes.

'Your Majesties…' The first person in line—a world-weary-looking woman—greeted them with a curtsey. Vasili extended his hand. The woman shook it with ill-concealed hope.

'It is good to see you, Maria.' Helia smiled, holding both the woman's hands.

Vasili was taken aback by the familiarity between them. He wondered if Helia had volunteered here, and that was why she'd chosen this place for them to make their first appearance. She'd had a life before he'd plucked her from it, and she had shown so much kindness and consideration. It was a theory that made sense.

As they greeted the line of people, he noticed the warmth

with which they all received her. He placed a hand on the small of her back and hazarded a glance behind him. Andreas and Carissa stood further away, allowing all the attention to fall on the new King and Queen, but his private secretary had an inscrutable look on his face, and Vasili didn't understand how he couldn't show at least a little emotion, standing where they were.

'Shall we show you around?' Maria asked.

'Please…after you.' Vasili gestured ahead of him.

The outside had barely prepared him for the inside. It was clear they were doing the best they could, with the funds they had, but calling the place shabby was as generous as he could be. There was a large, outdated kitchen, a common area, and numerous bedrooms with two to three children sharing each. He was relieved to see a recreation room of sorts, but it was severely lacking. The offices weren't that much better.

Helia had told him that she wanted to help the forgotten people of Thalonia, and he hadn't really known who that could be. Now, he hated it that he had been blind to this side of his kingdom. All those years he'd spent rebelling against the crown in a way that served *him* he could have spent rebelling in a way that served others. It had always been obvious that the politicians favoured the wealthy, as had his parents. But he could have used his rebellion for good, and it angered him that he had been so ignorant. Angered him that he had been lectured on propriety in his behaviour as a royal, when a royal was meant to serve everyone. His family didn't do that.

'Is there somewhere we can discuss matters?' he asked Maria.

'Yes, of course.'

'We would like to speak with all of you as well,' Helia said to the other staff.

They were taken into a room with a large table and some boxes stacked against the wall.

'I apologise. We can't offer you a better meeting room. Unfortunately, we don't have much space.'

'No apologies are necessary,' he said. 'We're here to listen. It's obvious that you're struggling—where are the issues?'

Maria needed no further encouragement than Helia nodding at her to speak. It was amazing to watch her interact with these people. *His* people. He had been worried about how she would fare today, but he hadn't needed to be. She was warm and listened carefully to their grievances, interjecting only to clarify their points. She showed a patience that he was struggling with—because it seemed Maria had to manage too much. There wasn't a proper organisational structure that would benefit the orphanage or the children. Hardly any of them would achieve any kind of greatness simply because there were no avenues for their betterment. Most of the staff were volunteers. How did this help anyone?

Things had to change.

He was grateful to Helia for showing him what he had been blind to. She was promising Maria things would improve. A move that had Andreas scowling.

Upon re-entering the main building, they finally got to meet some of the children that this place helped. From babies who grasped his heart in their tiny little fists to teenagers who were far too jaded for their young years. He could tell that Carissa was pleased they would get pictures that she could spin into something wildly positive, but if it hadn't been for Helia's presence beside him he would have been completely untethered. Sucked into his disappointment and anger.

He pulled her closer. Wrapping an arm around her waist as they further spoke to the volunteers. He needed her near.

But just as he had the thought, she was whisked away—and it couldn't have made him happier to see her go.

A little hand clasped onto Helia's, and out the corner of her eye she saw several of the royal entourage step forward. With a single look she ordered them away—not even stopping to reflect on the fact that she had controlled everyone wordlessly—and allowed the little girl to pull her out of Vasili's embrace.

This excursion had clearly been a shock to him. She could feel his emotions radiate through him. Frustration, anger, disappointment… Despite what he believed, he was a good man, and she could only imagine what seeing this side of his kingdom was doing to him—which was why she'd remained so close.

For her, this visit was monumental. Helia was more at home here than she'd ever felt at the palace. This was where she'd grown up. Where she'd spent her free time. When Helia had turned eighteen and left, it had been to start a hopeful new life. But now, returning as Queen, it was to bring a hopeful future for them all. This place—these people—had given her a home when she had none. A place that was now giving others a home. Like the little girl now tugging her away, so she didn't feel bad for leaving her husband.

'Where are you taking me, Anastasia?'

'Come and see what we made.'

The little girl she was well acquainted with from her

volunteering led her over to a group of children sitting on the floor, playing with building blocks.

'We built a palace.'

Anastasia tugged at Helia to join them on the floor, and she kneeled on the threadbare carpet. Andreas—barely hiding his displeasure—and several others looked as if they wanted to intervene.

'Stop,' Vasili commanded them.

She locked eyes with her husband, thinking the admonishment was for her, but there was something shifting in his gaze she couldn't decipher. There was a thread between them, and it went taut as he approached her. She watched him sit on a nearby couch, her heart full to bursting, as he examined the plastic brick construction.

'It's where you live,' one of Anastasia's little friends piped up.

'I think this is far more impressive than where I live,' she replied making the child's face light up.

'If this is Queen Helia's palace,' Vasili said, picking up a few stray bricks, 'then it needs a very big library.'

His eyes flashed to hers and her heart skipped a beat. She could feel heat creep up her neck. A heavy ache in her core that she had to hide. But he saw it. She knew by the small smirk on his face which he disguised with a broad smile for the others in their presence.

The feeling didn't go away in the time she and Vasili spent with the children. It meant more than she could say when he spoke to the older kids, who had tried to stay away, and within these walls where hope so often burned and died, Helia found herself hoping. Wishing she could have more with Vasili. With her husband who clearly cared for these people. *Her* people. And a deep sense of affection for him overcame her, flaring bright, but was quickly doused with an acute loneliness as she remembered all they were and all they could never be.

'We will be in touch. In the meantime, if you require anything contact our staff and it will be yours,' Vasili said, shaking Maria's hand.

'I promise things will get better.' Helia hugged the woman that she had known for most of her life and left with Vasili holding her close.

He remained silent on the drive back to the palace. Physically, he kept close to her. And a jolt of electricity passed through her at their every touch. But it seemed he was withdrawing into his thoughts, and she didn't like that. He had taken the title despite wanting to abdicate—a choice made for his people. Helia hadn't known how much of Thalonia's suffering he'd been aware of before, but seeing the look on his face when they'd toured the orphanage had answered that. He was her ally in this quest, so she needed to know what he was thinking.

'Are you okay?'

'You're asking me if *I'm* okay?'

She could see something flicker in his eyes before he sighed.

'No, Helia, I'm not. I didn't know it was this bad.' He rubbed his eyes with his thumb and finger. 'I should have. I was always aware of how much my family favoured those with power. Wealth. But I never stopped to consider what that would mean for others.'

'Maybe that's true—but, Vasili, we are doing something about it *now*. Those people back there were happy to see you for a reason.'

He huffed a humourless laugh. 'Don't try to placate me, Helia.'

'I'm not. I'm just telling you what I saw.'

She couldn't understand why he wouldn't acknowledge how much his words and actions meant to the people at the orphanage, but there wasn't much more time to dwell on it before they had arrived back at the palace.

They made their way to Vasili's office for the debrief that would follow. She'd expected both Andreas and Carissa to appear. However, it was only Andreas who did, wearing a deep scowl.

'I'm sure you have an opinion about today, Andreas, but let's recognise that it was a success,' Vasili said.

'I won't deny that Carissa will have what she needs to introduce you both to the world, sir,' Andreas said stiffly.

He was not happy, but Helia couldn't possibly imagine what could have set him off. She had remembered everything she needed to. Plus, Vasili had pledged his assistance, and it was the start of what she wanted to achieve.

Andreas turned to her. 'But *you*, Your Majesty, did not act in a way befitting of a queen.'

Helia could feel her buoyant mood dissipating. The high was gone and instead she was plunging back to earth. She thought she had done well. How could she have read the situation so wrong?

'I did everything expected of me,' Helia defended, recognising that she shouldn't have to, but also that Andreas knew so much more than she did. He had so much power over the staff and the politicians.

She'd fought to keep the steel in her voice, and felt Vasili move to stand at her back. She so badly wanted to lean on him now, but that would show weakness. Something she was not. She had given up her career, sacrificed everything for this mission. She would lean on no one.

'Meeting in a storeroom. Making promises that we don't know if we can keep. *Sitting on the floor.*'

Andreas's cheeks flared pink. Oh, he was angry.

'Never in all my years has any royal done that. We are meant to show strength. That we bow to no one. And yet you behaved like one of those ordinary volunteers. You acted without thought.'

He was right. She had acted without thought. She'd seen those children and seen herself in them. She hadn't felt like a queen when she'd played with them—she'd been just Helia. A woman who cared so much that she would say goodbye to the one thing she loved for them. Queens didn't do that. Queens found solutions that didn't affect them personally. But how could she do that when that very place was her past?

'You are not one of them any longer. You are Queen Helia Leos and you need to start behaving as such.'

'Enough.'

The gruff voice had come from beside her. There was a warm hand on her back, grounding her. Andreas fell silent.

'That's quite enough, Andreas. Leave us—and for your own sake, I suggest you do so quietly.'

Helia watched him march angrily through the door and once he was gone she turned to Vasili.

'You behaved like those ordinary volunteers.'

What if she had embarrassed Vasili? She relied on him to help her with this cause. What was more, things had been going well. She was growing to care for him more and more with each day. She couldn't bear the thought of hurting him in any way. She had to apologise.

'Vasili, I'm so—'

He cradled her face, seizing her lips, cutting off her apology with a hard kiss that had her letting out an unexpected moan. His tongue plunged into her mouth, setting off an avalanche of arousal through her body. She gasped as Vasili hooked his hands under her thighs and lifted her, setting her on the edge of his desk, making her just a little taller. Flame licked at the base of her spine as he stepped between her legs, deepening the kiss. He tasted of mint. The scent of his aftershave—cool and fresh, with something spicier that she could only describe as *his* scent—wrapped around her, chasing the apology from her mind. But she had to make it.

She pushed at his chest and he stopped immediately, his lips reluctantly leaving hers.

'Vasili, I have to say this—'

'No, you don't.' His voice was low. Rough. 'Don't you dare apologise.'

'But Andreas—'

'I don't care what Andreas said. All I saw today was a woman who cares.' He pressed a soft kiss to her lips. 'And I've wanted to kiss you all day.'

'Then do it.'

Vasili leaned in. Taking her lip between his teeth. Watching the way her eyes fluttered closed. He brushed his lips against hers, licking the seam of them, taking his time. Stoking the fire between them.

Seeing Helia interact with everyone at the orphanage had done something to his heart. He didn't care what his advisors said. The woman before him was the Queen this kingdom needed. He had wanted to kiss her then, a million times over, but he hadn't been able to. Their passion was behind closed doors. That was the agreement. But the need in him had built and built. Now, the noises she made as he tasted her had him growing hard. But he couldn't stop kissing her. He trailed kisses and bites down her neck, marking her. Everyone would see it. He would see it. It was a primitive thing to want to mark one's territory, but he couldn't care less. Especially when she called his name in that breathy way that satisfied something deep within.

Vasili recognised that he needed to step away from her for a moment or he would have his queen laid out on his desk.

He picked her up and carried her over to the couch, where he settled her on his lap, tucking her head against his shoulder. While he knew he needed to clear his head of the lusty haze, he didn't want to let her go. Not yet. He still had questions, and while they had privacy he was going to ask them.

'I need to thank you, Helia.'

'For what?'

'Showing me how we've failed.'

'Vasili…'

He looked down into her bright turquoise eyes. Her hand came up to his cheek and he laid his over hers. At first he thought he was going to remove it, but that wasn't possible. He craved her touch too much.

'*You* haven't failed at anything,' she said. 'Not yet, at least. You didn't run this kingdom before.'

'I could have done something sooner. I rebelled selfishly. Don't excuse my actions.'

He was angry at himself. So angry for not having bothered to look further than his own suffering.

'I'm not. But you saw something that was wrong today, and instead of making excuses you listened to them. You offered them help.'

But he needed to do more. And he still needed to know why it meant so much to Helia.

'As did you.'

'It's different for me,' she admitted.

'Why? Why is the orphanage so important to you? Why choose that for our first outing today? Andreas was right in that you could have picked something easier—not better, but certainly easier. I need to understand. Is this why you agreed to marry me?'

Helia pulled her hand from his face and glanced away, making Vasili worry that he had pushed too soon. But he needed to know. He felt Helia's chest expand as she took a deep breath, and without looking at him she started speaking in a low voice that failed to hide her pain.

'I grew up there.'

Which explained why she'd been received so warmly. She was one of them.

'I was barely a teenager when my father died, and with my mother having passed away long before, my Uncle Giannis became my guardian. They were close, Giannis and my father. They were business partners. My father was the creative one. He was warm and kind and people loved his flower arrangements. Giannis was the opposite. Coldly logical. He was great at business and finance, so their partnership worked well. My father had made him executor of his estate.'

Vasili had a bad feeling he knew where this was going.

'My father had left the business to Giannis. It employed enough florists that it would still make money without him, but he'd also left a monetary inheritance for me. A substantial amount. It would have taken care of me. Helped me study. Get a start in life.'

The light flowing through the large windows sparkled on a tear as it fell, kissing her cheek before disappearing. Vasili brushed the wetness away and wrapped his arms around her.

'I went to stay with Giannis. He had always been nice

to me when my father was alive, but he changed. He became cruel. He would tell me that I was a burden. That he
hadn't wanted a family and what made me enough reason
to change that about his life? I tried so hard to be good.
To make sure he didn't notice me more than he needed to.
I would do chores, and try to cook, but nothing I did was
good enough. I missed my father and my uncle was awful.
Maybe he had always been that way and everything else
was an act. I don't know. Anyway, he dealt with the law-
yers and the banks and everything else. I was at the will-
reading, so I knew I was getting an inheritance. What I
didn't know was that Giannis had opened a bank account
for me and he had full signing rights on it because I was a
minor. My inheritance was paid into it, and once the estate
was settled he moved every penny into his own account.
He said it was what he was owed and then he packed me a
suitcase—just one—and dropped me off at the orphanage.'

Vasili tightened his arms around her, trying very hard to
rein in his temper. He wanted to find Giannis Demetriou
and make him pay for his sins. For making Helia question
her worth.

'Maria was the director back then too. She tried to get
me to make friends with the others, but I couldn't. I withdrew from everyone.'

Vasili didn't blame her. She had been abandoned—why
would she want to trust anyone? He could understand that.

It dawned on him that she was trusting him enough to
tell him her story. Vasili had never been protective of anything, but now, as he listened to Helia's story, the need to
protect flared blindingly bright in him. He wanted to shield
her. Keep her safe from everyone and everything. Nothing
would touch her again. He vowed it in that moment.

'I had to change schools. A forgotten little school with a

terribly small library. But it was something. The librarian there let me help out, and slowly things got better. I knew then that a librarian was what I wanted to be—but you saw what it's like at the orphanage. It's only the fortunate ones who go on to achieve their dreams. I swore that one day I would find a way to help them...which is why I volunteer there when I can. But have always wanted to do more.'

Vasili hadn't thought he could get any angrier, but here he was, trying to hide his trembling from Helia. The crown hadn't done enough. Not for people like Helia. Not for those having to live away from the bright lights of Seidon. His family had failed for generations.

He kissed her temple, cradling her to his body. He could have told her that he was sorry she'd had to go through that—because he was. He could have told her he wanted vengeance in her name—because he did. But he didn't say any of that because he couldn't change the past.

Instead, he said, 'Helia, I am King of Thalonia and you are my queen and together we will fix this. We will fix what's broken in this kingdom so that no one else will have to endure what you did. No one will be forgotten while we rule.'

'Vasili...' she breathed, in a way that stopped his heart.

With eyes full of tears she kissed him. Tugging on his hair as she pulled him closer. He lifted her and placed her over him to straddle his lap, letting her control this frantic kiss until he wanted more.

He threaded his fingers in her hair, angling his head so he could kiss her more deeply, and then he pulled away for just a breath. 'I escaped into books too.'

Helia laughed against his lips. The single most joyous sound after her tears had cut through him. His lips were back on hers instantly. Something molten was stirring within him. Scorching him with every pass of their lips. And then his hands trailed down her body, digging into her soft flesh as the overwhelming need to be buried inside her gripped him in an iron hold. He dragged Helia's hips forward. Her core brushed against his hardness, making him moan. Low. Deep. He flexed against her, driving them both mad.

Crazed. That was how he felt. All he could think of was more.

'Helia…' he groaned, biting her chin, her throat.

He slipped his hands under her dress and knew she would be slick for him. How easy it would be to shed these clothes, these flimsy fabric barriers, and push into her.

Her sighs and mewls had every link on the chains he had around himself breaking apart. He wanted her. Now.

His fingers tightened around the band of her panties. He could tear them right off her. Feel her warmth against his skin. Feel her clench around him.

No! a voice at the back of his mind shouted.

What was he doing? He couldn't have sex with her. Especially not now, when they were both raw. He couldn't let them seek comfort in each other like that. Not to mention he had no protection.

Vasili tore his lips away from Helia's and pressed his forehead against hers. Their breaths were ragged. He had been so close to forsaking his mission. The thought of what might have happened if he'd entered her bare was sobering. He couldn't risk having a child. The throne wasn't meant to endure. But he had found Helia so tempting he had forgotten what he was working towards.

'I'm sorry…' he panted.

'For what?'

Her pupils were blown wide. Skin flushed. How wonderful it would be to see her writhing under him.

'This isn't what you need right now. Not after what you told me.'

It was an excuse, and he knew it, but he couldn't tell her that he didn't want to have sex with her, because that would be a lie, and he couldn't tell her that they shouldn't, because he could barely remember why. But he could tell her he would take care of her—because he would.

'I'm not going to have sex with you, but I am going to take care of you. Allow me that?'

Helia studied his face. Searching, he presumed, for an answer he couldn't give her. And maybe she understood, because she nodded and shifted off him.

He stood and adjusted the evidence of his arousal, then took her hand, leading her out of the office. Their union wasn't meant to include sex, but he couldn't ignore their physical reaction to each other. And now he thought maybe there was more to it than that. Because every thought he had in this moment centred around his wife.

Vasili told himself that he had to do better…to remember why he held himself back. He couldn't lose control again.

CHAPTER TWELVE

VASILI HADN'T SLEPT a wink. All he'd been able to think about was what Helia had been through. He had known loneliness, but even though his family had never been there for him, he'd still had a brother who had cared to a degree. He hadn't been entirely abandoned—not like Helia. To trust someone, to think they had your best interests in mind, and then to be so betrayed at such a young age would have broken anyone. Especially at such a vulnerable time.

Vasili still didn't know how to react to the trust she had shown in telling him. He'd never had anyone wanting to be that close to him. Now the first person to do so was the one person he was trying to keep at arm's length, and it was proving harder and harder every day.

Having her confide in him had made him feel fulfilled in a way that was alien, even if it also angered him that she'd had to deal with so much strife.

At least now he understood why she'd married him. Why this mission of hers was so important. Seeing the people at the orphanage had affected him, but to know that Helia had been one of them both crushed him and ignited a determination to help her. Which was why he had finally given up on sleep and worked on the solution that he would propose to her. He would include her in every step.

As soon as the rest of the palace had awakened, he had sent for her.

For now he sat with Andreas, a folder open before him. He studied his advisor and personal secretary, who seemed hell-bent on pushing for a bill that went against everything Vasili was hoping to achieve. He kept one eye on the door. Helia would be arriving shortly. He could already picture her expression when she learnt about this.

'This does nothing to better Thalonia,' Vasili said, tossing a page back into the folder.

'Of course it does, Your Majesty. This would benefit everyone.'

'Everyone whom you deem important,' Vasili corrected. 'This is trickle-down economics.'

'Nothing is more effective.'

'Don't try to sell that to me, Andreas. We both know it doesn't work that way.'

'It's my advice to you to sign off on this bill.'

Vasili stared Andreas down. There was absolutely no way that he would. Bills like this were the reason why places like the orphanage existed in the state they did. Why the poor of Thalonia suffered in silence. His father would have signed off on it, but Vasili was determined on being a different kind of king.

Through the tension, a knock sounded on the door and in walked Helia. She was frowning as she looked between him and Andreas.

'What's going on here?'

It wasn't a tentative question; it was a demand to know.

Vasili could see how she was blossoming into her role even if she still doubted herself at times.

'It's nothing for you to be concerned about, Your Majesty,' Andreas said.

Vasili knew that tone. But disregarding Helia would never be something he accepted. His father had ruled absolutely. His mother, though she'd been Queen, had only ever been allowed power over things he'd deemed acceptable for her. Vasili had hated it then and he hated it now. Perhaps it was the rebellion in him which he probably would never be rid of. The need to do things his way.

Helia was his partner. They had agreed to show a united front to the world. That included his advisors, so as far as Vasili was concerned, and she would always have a voice.

Holding Andreas's stare, he slid the folder over to Helia, who had come to stand beside him. 'This is a proposed tax bill that I will not be passing.'

Helia read through the pages in the folder, grateful for her background as a librarian. All the knowledge she had absorbed over the years helped her understand the document in her hand now. One that made her heart sink. This was proof of the barriers she needed to overcome to ensure the people who needed help the most received it.

The one shining light was Vasili. He was already opposed. A fact that made her breathe a sigh of relief. The problem was Andreas was obviously pushing for it.

'I'm no expert, but to me this would only benefit those already wealthy. There is no benefit for the poor. They're likely to be forgotten. Seems like you're pushing for something only the upper echelons want,' she said evenly as she set the folder down.

'That is exactly it,' Vasili agreed.

Vasili had told her to wield her power. Had said to her numerous times that she was Queen. Reminded her when he kissed and touched her. And after their talk the day before it was finally starting to settle—because the only person whose opinion she should value was her husband's.

When they had returned from the orphanage Andreas's words had had her doubting herself. She could see that he didn't care for everyone. But she did. And Vasili did. So she would no longer allow him to make her feel as if her title was an ill fit.

'Vasili is right. We can't pass this. As Queen, I am opposed.'

Just as she had expected, Andreas did not take well to her statement.

'This is irregular. It is the King who has a say in the policy of our country. That was how King Athanasios did things, and that was how King Leander did as well.'

'It would appear that once again you need reminding, Andreas, that I am not my father, nor my brother. I will accept the counsel of my queen because she is the only one amongst us who is intimately aware of how our policies affect and fail the ordinary citizens of Thalonia. Helia has as much of a say in the wellbeing of our people as I do, and we are both opposed. If you want this bill passed in Parliament, I suggest it be reworked.'

While Vasili did not raise his voice, Helia was taken by the power in it. He might be a reluctant king, but to her he was already a good one.

She turned to Vasili as soon as Andreas had left and said, 'Thank you.'

'We agreed to fix things together, did we not?'

They had, and he was already following through on that promise. He treated her with consideration, valued her opinions, and it was making it so much harder for her to keep her feelings under lock and key. She was forbidden from falling in love. He didn't want them to fall in love. But he made it so hard. She already trusted him. He had asked for her trust in small ways, but had earned it in the biggest, which was why she had felt comfortable telling him of her past. Helia hadn't told anyone the whole truth, but she'd told Vasili, and it hadn't scared her to say it.

It was clear that she was well on her way to breaking her promise and losing her heart to him, but he would never do the same. How could he treat her so well, help her and listen to her, and then refuse to love her?

'We did.'

'But that isn't why I asked you here.' He stood and offered her his chair, pushing it in when she sat, then lifting the lid of his laptop. 'This is what I want to discuss with you.'

Helia skimmed through the document, her breath catching. 'When did you do this?'

'I couldn't sleep,' Vasili admitted, perching on the corner of the table, looking down at her. 'What do you think?'

'You want to make orphanages a palace concern.'

'Yes. That way we can secure funding that I get to dictate without having to go through the politicians. That's not all. I plan on creating an educational fund that the orphans will have access to for further study.'

'How would we make that work?'

'Possibly some sort of bursary fund.'

That would be perfect. She knew first-hand that not everyone shared in academic dreams, it would be a standout achievement for them to say that the palace had taken notice of them. It would give them the leg up in the world that they desperately needed.

'And for the orphanages?'

'Those funds would be dealt with separately, and with

your help I think I can come up with a framework to allocate resources fairly.'

With her help.

Not only was Vasili helping Helia achieve her mission far sooner than she had dared to hope, but he also wasn't taking it away from her. He wanted her to be a part of it. And that meant more than he would ever know.

'This is going to be a big project, Helia. Of course you would be part of it. After all, this is your mission.'

Helia felt a burning in her eyes, but she wouldn't allow herself to cry. It didn't matter that she was happy. She needed to keep her emotions at bay long enough to make it through the rest of the discussion. But she knew he was coming to understand her. Read her like no one else ever could.

'What's this about schools?' With all the emotion clogging up her throat, her voice came out strangled.

'That is my decree increasing the national spend on education.'

'Thank you, Vasili.'

'No, don't thank me. This change is long overdue. You and I…we're changing this kingdom, Helia. I will not be toeing any lines to keep people who have watched Thalonia suffer comfortable. We need new traditions.'

Helia didn't have words for how much this meant to her. Once she had taken him to the orphanage—only once. And this was what he had done. She couldn't contain herself any more…couldn't deny what she felt for him. Vasili was kind and considerate and caring, and she knew without a shadow of doubt right then that she was hopelessly in love with him.

Helia couldn't find the moment when it had happened, and realised she had fallen for him in little bits from the first time she'd met him. That was why she trusted him. Why she'd told him about her past. It was because she loved him.

Without thinking, she flung herself at Vasili and kissed him. He didn't hesitate, not even for second, and he kissed her back.

Hands on her waist, he held her firm as she wrapped her arms around his neck. Lightning crackled through her veins as his tongue delved into her mouth, stroking her. Making her come alive. Then he spun them around, placing her on the large desk, and moved to stand between her legs. She cursed the tailored trousers she wore, because she wanted to feel the warm hand that was travelling up the outside of her thigh.

She wanted him to lay her down on the desk and feast on her. She wanted to show him with her body what he meant to her because she couldn't say the words.

Helia wrapped her legs around him, sinking her hands under his jacket. Scratching down his sides over his perfectly starched white shirt. She felt the muscles beneath her fingers tense.

'Helia…'

He moaned out her name and angled his head, kissing her deeper. Wilder. And she wanted this. She wanted him to break free with her. He was only barely managing to restrain himself. She felt it in the tremor of his arms and the scrape of his teeth. It awakened such a wild desire, which was only further fuelled by the torrent of love within her.

'Vasili…' she breathed into his ear.

He cursed, pulling her hips to the edge of the table, grinding his hardness against her core.

Her whimper sent shockwaves of lust racing through him.

He couldn't stop this time.

Vasili realised that when it came to Helia, he wasn't the

one in control. And he was tired. So tired of wanting and not having. So tired of the rebellion that had given him choice but taken just as much away.

Choosing Helia had been a rebellion, but denying himself his need to take her to bed was a rebellion too. A rebellion against his need for her. He hadn't forgotten why he didn't want to have sex with her, but he was losing his grasp on his willpower and the want coursing through him strangled him.

For once he wanted to ignore everything else and take what would make him happy.

'Let go with me,' she told him.

He wanted to. He was barely hanging on by a thread. The hold on his barriers was beyond tenuous now. All he wanted was to be deep inside her.

'Is this what you want?'

He gritted out the question, hoping she would say no. He needed her to, because she was the only thing that could stop them now. And yet he was praying she would say yes, because he wanted her so badly he couldn't think straight.

'Yes.'

It was the key that unlocked every shackle on him. He had nothing left in him to resist her any more. He only prayed that this would not be his ruination.

She tugged him even closer to her, but he shook his head. He wouldn't allow their first time like this to be a rushed, torrid affair on his office desk.

He placed a gentle kiss on her lips, then took her hand and led her from the office.

Vasili walked right past their shared bedroom. He didn't want her there. He was taking her to what was his room. His quiet sanctum.

He shut the door, not giving her a chance to look at their

surroundings before his lips were on hers again, and without breaking their kiss he picked Helia up. Her legs wrapped around him without him having to tell her.

Vasili didn't want to think of what this would mean for them. He didn't want to think of why it seemed that they danced perfectly in sync with each other. All he wanted was to lose himself in her.

He pressed her back against the closed door. His breath hissed from his lips as he pushed his hardness against her. Her gasp was music to him. The sweetest sound.

'Please, Vasili, I need you.'

He needed her too, with an urgency that defied all thought or logic. But there was no room for thought. Not now.

With sure steps he crossed the room and laid her gently upon the bed. Seeing her lying on his dark sheets, staring back at him with hooded eyes, he felt a savage sort of possessiveness overcome him.

This woman—his queen, a goddess—was his.

But she had been so timid when they had first become intimate... He needed to know just how inexperienced she was.

'Have you done this before, Helia?' He kneeled over her, supporting himself on a muscular arm beside her head.

Her skin burned red. 'Yes, but—'

'But?'

'It doesn't matter.' She looked away.

Holding her chin in his fingers, he forced her to meet his gaze. 'It does to me. Honesty. Remember?'

'I had sex with someone I had dated, but it wasn't enjoyable. It was always uncomfortable. And after him I avoided it even if I wanted it. I couldn't let go. I couldn't allow myself to trust.'

Anger burned alongside Vasili's lust. He couldn't do anything to change her past experience, but he would make sure she knew only pleasure now.

'I won't hurt you.'

'I know.'

He ran his hand along the side of her body. 'Let me show you how a king worships you.'

'A king doesn't worship a queen.'

She ran her fingers through his hair. He caught her wrist and kissed her palm. 'A king worships a goddess.'

And that was what he wanted to do. For weeks she had haunted his thoughts and dreams.

'I have wanted you for so long, Helia. I've dreamt of this moment. Of what you will feel like when I sink into you.'

'What did you do in your dreams?'

'I peeled every maddening layer of cloth from your body. Slowly. Until you wanted to tear them off yourself.'

With his teeth, Vasili pulled down the zipper on her trousers, never taking his eyes off her. He kissed the lace peeking between the parted fabric and peeled it off her legs. Her breath was coming in heavy pants.

He kissed his way up her body, running his lips over her neck, making her shiver as he undid the buttons on her blouse. She clutched at the sheets. At her hair.

'Just like this,' he whispered in her ear, only to draw away and remove the rest of her clothing with the same teasing slowness until her pupils had swallowed up most of the turquoise in her eyes. 'And then I kissed you.'

He brushed his lips over hers, then took her mouth hungrily. Teasing Helia like this had unleashed a firestorm of want within him, but he didn't care about his need for release because he craved seeing Helia come apart for him. The sight was addictive.

He broke the kiss, pulling away, and he chuckled when Helia tried to follow. He kept her down on the bed, saying, 'But not here.'

'Where?'

He grinned as he settled between her legs, seeing her slickness on her golden skin, and lowered his mouth to her mound. His tongue slid through her folds as he kissed her deeply. He became lost in her taste and her scent and the symphony of her moans as he made her soar further, higher, until she reached her release with a keening cry, sobbing his name.

He kissed every inch of her body, sucking her nipples into his mouth, marking her perfect skin with his teeth, drawing out her pleasure until she calmed, and then he kept going until she was panting once more.

Vasili shucked off his clothes and reached into a drawer, retrieving a foil square. He saw Helia's eyes follow him.

'Vasili, I'm on birth control.'

'I'm glad to hear it,' he said, brushing his fingers through her caramel curls.

He truthfully was glad, but accidents did happen, and even though he wanted nothing more than to feel Helia around him, he was determined that they would never have heirs. He couldn't. So he ripped open the packet and rolled the protection along his length.

And then he had Helia's hips in his hands, spreading her thighs apart so he could see himself sinking into her. A hurricane of pleasure consumed him. Stealing his breath. Grabbing his heart in a fist.

She felt like heaven. Like everything he had known she would and so much more.

He cursed on a breath. 'Helia…'

This was so much more overwhelming than Vasili had

anticipated. It felt too good—and not just in the way the pleasure rolled over him in unending waves. It felt too much like home. As if being with Helia like this was fated.

Vasili had crossed a boundary he knew he shouldn't have. Because he would never want to stop doing this with her. It was exactly as he had feared.

CHAPTER THIRTEEN

VASILI HAD MADE her wait for this and it was worth every minute. With him sliding in and out of her, Helia's voice flowed from her in unintelligible moans. None of her fantasies compared. She hadn't ever felt current like this in her body, this heat in her veins and a coiling deep in her core. And then there was Vasili. The sheen of sweat on his sculpted torso. The look of ecstasy on his face. There was also vulnerability there. Something he would normally cover up. But he couldn't now.

'More…' she begged, and he obliged.

Wrapping his arms tightly around her body, he fused them together. His thrusts were growing harder. Faster. His breaths were coming in a constant rapid rush. She had thought it couldn't possibly feel better than it had when he'd had his mouth on her, but *this* was all-consuming.

She lost her whole heart to him. Feeling utter pleasure. Treasured. Protected.

His rhythm was growing erratic as he drew close to release and Helia was right there with him. Stretching. Coiling. Reaching for her peak. And as he slammed his hips into her, tensing as he spilled, she shattered around him. Calling his name as he dropped his head into the crook of her neck and they rode out their pleasure together.

'Helia...'

Everything had changed. She felt it. Heard it in his voice. They had crossed over to somewhere new. Except she didn't know where that was. What it would mean for them. For her and this new, pulsing love that thrummed faster than her heart.

'Don't move.'

Vasili kissed her forehead, then disappeared into the bathroom to dispose of the condom. She heard running water and he returned with a warm towel that he used to clean her up. Then he tossed it aside and drew her into his arms.

By now Helia had lain in his arms numerous times, but this time it was so different. She turned towards him and Vasili held her against his hard body. She kissed the base of his throat, knowing that her heart was his. She loved him, but she couldn't say it.

Helia looked into his face and saw that every one of the barriers he had erected around him had come crashing down. She didn't know how long it would last, but for the moment at least he was hers.

So she settled into his embrace and looked at their surroundings. At the modern room and the books and the art.

'I've finally found a place in this palace that looks like you belong in it,' she said.

'Is that so?'

Helia was coming to understand Vasili. She could tell when he was trying to cover up his feelings.

'Yes. The title suits you. You are the King, Vasili. But that office doesn't suit you.' She kissed him lightly on the lips. 'You should make it yours. Like it is here.'

His arms tightened around her. She felt his lips on the top of her head.

'I was barely out of my teens when I ordered the change. I needed somewhere to belong.'

Soft words that had the power to break a heart. Helia wanted to ease the hurt in him, but to do that she needed him to open up to her.

'What was it like growing up here? Being a prince?'

'Lonely. The only reason my parents had me was because they had to have a spare. Nannies raised me from as far back as I can remember. Well, one did.'

'What was she like?'

Vasili smiled. Sad, yet fond. His eyes were focused on some faraway place. 'Sophia was…warm. She was funny and playful. Kind. Smarter than anyone gave her credit for. And she took care solely of me.'

'You two must have been close.'

'We were.'

There was a gruffness in his voice that had Helia trying to move even closer to him. Trying to soothe an old hurt.

'Until my parents ordered that she be fired when I turned fifteen. She said nothing to them. Refused to report to Andreas or thank anyone for having worked here. She broke all the rules of propriety by addressing only me before she left. She told me never to bow.'

Helia could see the connection between Vasili and Sophia. Kind, rebellious souls. 'Do you know where she went?'

'No, I wasn't allowed to look for her. Not until recently, when I found that she had passed away a few years ago.'

'That's awful. I'm sorry.'

Helia could only imagine how hard it would have been for him to lose the person closest to him because she had been taken away. Forced to abandon him.

'There's a lot of that in these walls, Helia,' he said, matter-of-factly.

'You couldn't lean on Leander either,' she said, speaking her thoughts out loud.

Vasili sighed. 'I was ordered by my parents not to waste Leander's time. He was being raised to be King, so I kept my distance as much as I could.'

'Except at night.'

She remembered his story from the beach, and thinking then that he had in fact been close with his brother, but maybe Vasili had never got to have the relationship with him he wanted.

'Yes.' He chuckled. A low rumble in his chest. 'We once stole an entire tart. Sophia found it the next day.'

Helia laughed. 'Did you get in trouble?'

'No,' Vasili said, as if the idea was preposterous. 'We ate a little more of it before she got rid of the evidence. I couldn't get in trouble.'

'Because you were the Prince?'

'Because someone has to care, and as long as I stayed out of the way no one did.'

'But your parents—'

'Were the King and Queen of Thalonia and had no time for me. I was an insurance policy, Helia. Nothing more than that. Being their son or behaving perfectly—none of it was worth anything. I wasn't worth their affection.'

Helia had never felt such anger towards people she'd been supposed to admire. Andreas had told her how Vasili's parents had been loved throughout the Kingdom. The perfect monarchs. She wanted to laugh. How could they have been perfect monarchs, people meant to care for an entire kingdom, when they hadn't even cared for their own child.

Her heart ached for the young boy alone in this big palace.

Alone.

Lonely.

Just like her.

'How did you cope?'

It was hard to comprehend that someone who had every right to be angry and cold was anything but.

'I told you—I rebelled. At first I would escape into the library and books...'

Helia had spied the stack on the bedside table. She couldn't help but think it was a sign of a deeper connection between them.

'Afterwards I acted out. Rebelled against the idea of being the perfect son. The perfect prince. I didn't want to be a prince at all. The partying, sex, women—all seemed to get a bigger reaction. And since all I wanted was to live my life, I figured living hard was a win all round.'

'But it didn't make you happy.'

'No, it didn't. And I regret my choice of rebellion now.'

Helia looked into his face then, attempting to read his thoughts. 'Why?'

'Because seeing the other side of Seidon...the orphanage... I knew I could have done something real.'

'This world is not made up of good people. It's full of people like me.'

But he was good. Vasili was better than he realised. He had been hurt over and over by the people who should have loved him most. He hadn't seen love from his family, and the one person who had loved him was taken away. So Helia understood why he'd told her he didn't love, but knew he was blind to all the ways in which he showed that he did.

'It's why I don't blame the people for wishing Leander was still on the throne. I'm sure they would rather our places had been switched.'

Helia looked up at him, horrified. 'Surely you don't believe that!'

He said nothing.

'Is that what you think? That it would have been better if you were on that plane?'

More silence.

A knot formed in Helia's throat. He really was an island. Alone at sea with all his hurt. So much so that she was certain he didn't even love himself.

'Vasili, look at me.'

He looked down at her, his normally bright, intelligent eyes showing nothing at all. They were perfectly expressionless and she hated it.

'You didn't know. And now that you do, you have a plan to fix things. You are helping me with the thing that means the most to me. You are good and kind and your people love you. I hate what your parents did to you, but it's their loss. Do you hear me? You were and are entitled to the way you feel. You are entitled to affection.'

'Helia…' he said in a low voice.

'Do you hear me?'

He huffed a laugh and kissed her lightly. 'I hear you.'

'Good.'

She was quiet for a moment, thinking through everything he'd revealed to her. She completely understood why he didn't want to be King, but she had no doubt he was the King Thalonia needed. She also finally understood why he was so set against having children. In his place, she would feel the same.

'You not wanting heirs…is that the reason you held back?'

'It's not that I don't want children, Helia, it's that I know what kind of life awaits them if I do. I won't do that.'

'No, you won't. Because it's not in you to be cruel.'

She remembered how good he'd been with the children

at the orphanage. Every one of them. Yet he thought he wasn't good. Helia wouldn't allow it. She'd noticed that he avoided her question, which meant not having children wasn't the reason he tried to keep his distance. She considered that maybe this lonely, unloved boy still couldn't trust anyone to be in his corner. She certainly hadn't until Vasili came along.

Whatever he thought, Vasili needed love. And lying on his bed, in his arms, Helia vowed that she would be strong enough to love him. Even if it meant he could never return it. Even if she craved hearing the words he might never be able to say, she would love him still.

She was risking her heart, but that already belonged to him. It did scare her that Vasili was the first person she'd admitted to loving since losing her father. If he ever found out how she felt he might decide to abandon her too. But there was absolutely no way she would allow Vasili to feel that he didn't deserve love or had to earn it.

He was enough, and she would show him. Even though her heart was further fracturing at the thought of how lonely it would be to spend a lifetime in this vortex of un-requited love.

CHAPTER FOURTEEN

HELIA WALKED DOWN a golden lit passage. Her dress swished along the marble floors. She barely felt her arm in her husband's as she reflected on the days and weeks that had followed their first time together. They'd been some of the best and the worst. But each day had started with them wrapped around one another and ended the same way. Each day she'd felt stronger. Settling in her role as Queen.

After the clash with Andreas over the tax bill, things had improved with him as well. Perhaps he was coming to accept how different the new King and Queen were, but Helia didn't know for sure. What she did know was that since then she had dealt with him with an authority that sometimes felt uncomfortable, but was always fuelled by her pursuit of her goals.

She and Vasili went about their duties, made their appearances together and apart, and worked on their project. They were achieving many of their objectives quickly.

She read a different story about her and Vasili every other day in the media, and they were all greatly positive. The people liked it that she was one of the masses, now a queen.

Yet every day felt harder.

Every day she would love her husband. Show him that

she did but never utter the words. Every day that one-sided affection had her growing lonelier. And when she looked to the future all she saw was this path stretching on. Just her and Vasili, stuck in this magical, desolate connection.

Vasili didn't want children, and she had knowingly agreed to his terms, so that meant she would have no family—ever. No outlet for all the love inside her. No one to want and need her as much as she wanted and needed them.

Helia only realised they had arrived at their destination when she was jerked to a stop.

'You seem distracted,' Vasili said.

Helia looked at the shut double doors and shook her head, keeping her every thought well hidden. 'Just a lot on my mind.'

Of course she would be nervous about the coronation banquet. Vasili thought to himself.

It would be her first interaction with foreign dignitaries. He didn't want to be here either. His reasons for hating the event hadn't changed, but he had resigned himself to doing his duty.

Even as he'd walked down the passage with Helia on his arm he'd still been wishing he didn't have to step through these gilded doors, but this tradition served a purpose.

'If it helps, think of it less as a celebration and more as an opportunity to meet everyone as King,' Helia offered.

There would be politics to navigate. Every word more than it seemed. Alliances and threats made with smiles on faces and warm hands to shake.

Vasili hooked a hand around Helia's nape, pulling her in for a kiss that heated his blood as it always did.

'I wasn't prepared to wait.'

Especially when she looked so beautiful. Soft and feminine in a pale blue dress falling in layers of chiffon and tulle that reminded him of flowing water. Her hair was pinned up at the centre of her crown, an heirloom of diamonds and sapphires donned by every queen at the coronation banquet. And on her finger sat his ring.

She placed her hand over his heart, on the gold sash that sat on his black uniform. He thought she looked like the very heart of the Kingdom, and if she was its heart he had to be its immovable pillar of strength.

Helia laughed. 'You never are.'

'Ready?'

When she nodded, the doors to the ballroom swung open and in they walked to a room full of splendour. Gold and frescoed walls. Elaborate floral arrangements atop tall pillars. Gentle music flowing from the string quintet.

It was also a room filled with people. Royalty, dignitaries, politicians, billionaires…so much power, so much influence in one place.

They were announced, and then it began. Introductions and handshakes. Pleasantries and carefully worded welcomes that didn't sound welcoming at all.

Once they'd made their way around the room, Vasili excused them and spun Helia onto the floor. It was an invitation for everyone to join them in dance. But Vasili didn't care about that. He just wanted his wife in his arms.

'Everyone is looking at us…it takes a little getting used to,' Helia said as she placed her free hand on his shoulder.

With his palm on the small of her back, he tugged her a little closer, leading her through the ebb and flow of the swirling melody. Perfectly in sync.

'I'm not surprised that they're looking.' He bent low,

pressing a kiss to her cheek. 'I have the most beautiful woman in my arms.'

He smiled at her blush. Helia had shown such strength and intelligence in the weeks since they had married. She was a force in her own right, but he still loved being able to make her blush and then watch her go from blushing to being demanding and enthusiastic in bed. He got to see all the many facets of Helia, and he wasn't sure he deserved the privilege.

But now he knew what everyone else would be seeing. He could feel it between them. An energy that caught everything around them. The current in their touch and the electricity in the air.

'I want to take you to bed and have my way with you.'

Helia wrapped her arms around his neck, pulling herself closer until her lips were at his ear. She said, 'Well, you're just going to have to be patient, Your Majesty.'

'Not a virtue of mine. In fact, I'm not very virtuous at all—you should know that by now.'

'What I know,' she said slowly, 'is that the longer I keep you waiting, the happier I'll be later.'

'Tease…'

'You wouldn't have it any other way.'

She pulled away from his embrace and with a sly smile over her shoulder made her way back through the crowd. She was right—he wouldn't have it any other way. She was perfect, and somehow she managed to make him feel lighter than he ever had before. Somehow she managed to help him not just to accept being King, but to like it. She had opened his eyes, and now he had the power to effect change.

Vasili kept an eye on Helia even as he was drawn into group after group of guests. After what seemed like the thousandth conversation along similar lines, he lost sight of her.

She was still within the palace walls. Safe. But he couldn't ignore the way her absence grated on him. It was ridiculous when he had known her for such a short time.

'She's doing well tonight,' he heard Andreas say beside him.

Vasili wondered what it had cost Andreas to admit that. 'Yes, she is. She has been all along.'

He glanced at his private secretary knowing he wouldn't get any response. It was then that the crowd parted, and he caught sight of her with the Queen of a neighbouring island kingdom. As if she had a sixth sense for where he was, she turned and smiled at him from across the room, never once halting in her conversation.

He wanted her back by his side, so with sure steps Vasili crossed the room.

'I'm sorry to interrupt, but I need to steal my wife away.'

Vasili slipped his arm around Helia's waist, pulling her closer in a move that was unapologetically possessive. It was not missed by the woman in their company.

'My apologies, Queen Arianna,' said Helia. 'It was lovely to meet you.'

The visiting Queen smiled in a knowing way, waving off Helia's apology. 'I too was once young and in love. I hope to see you soon.'

Vasili heard Helia promise that she would, but his mind was firmly fixed on that one word. *Love.* It wasn't love that he felt. He didn't love. It wasn't possible to feel something one knew nothing about. What he and Helia had was pure passion.

He led Helia out onto the cool, brightly lit balcony. Soon

he was kissing her with an urgency that she returned. Proof that he was right.

Helia frowned at him when they broke apart, a question in her eyes, but before he could address it, they were being approached by a group of men he hadn't thought of in weeks. Hadn't heard from or contacted.

'Vasili,' his friend Stavros greeted him.

'*King* Vasili,' another corrected.

'We haven't seen you in a while.' His friend snapped his gaze to Helia. 'But I guess you have been busy. Your Majesty.'

Stavros inclined his head, a familiar smirk painted on his lips. It had never bothered Vasili before, but now he wanted to shove Helia behind him. Be her shield until the lot of them left.

'It's a pleasure to meet you,' Helia said pleasantly.

No, it was not. Not to him. These were the people he'd partied with. Nobility. Members of the highest echelons of society. But he couldn't deny he hated seeing Helia interact with them.

'Why so tense, Your Majesty?' Stavros asked.

Normally the man's inability to take anything seriously entertained him. Not today.

Vasili pressed Helia further into his side. 'Maybe I don't like you talking to my wife.'

'Territorial?' Stavros laughed.

Anger bloomed in his chest. Not at Stavros, but at himself. Because the man was right. Vasili didn't like seeing Helia with these people because they reflected the ugliest parts of himself. He was selfish. Not worthy of anything meaningful. The women of before had known not to expect a relationship with him. He hadn't cared about their feelings. He'd been out for a good time. Which made him no better than Stavros or any of the men now talking to his wife. They weren't his friends. He didn't have any of those. None of these people had contacted him after Leander's death. None of them had reached out when he had married or taken the throne.

And he hadn't missed any of them.

Realisation dawned that he wasn't even worthy of the most superficial, disposable affection. Of affection of any sort. He had learned that over and over with his parents and now he learned it again.

'You're damn right, I am.'

'Never thought I'd see the day...'

Helia was no longer paying attention to the group of men they were talking to. Her heart had hammered in her chest as Stavros's words had landed. Vasili had lived a very different life from her own. He had been with women so unlike her. None of whom he felt anything for. And even though she was his wife, she wasn't any different—because now she was in his bed. She got to enjoy his touches and his attention, and to a certain degree, his support. But nothing more.

'I too was once young and in love.'

Except Queen Arianna was wrong. Vasili didn't love her. *She* had been the one to break the rules. *She* had been the one to fall in love. And all she'd got in return was an increasingly lonely existence. Because she realised now that she had always craved having someone to love and to love her back. She wanted Vasili to love her back...but he had said so many times that he couldn't do that.

She didn't want to spend her life pining for the man in her bed, wanting him in a way that she couldn't have. She wanted more.

And in that moment her crown fell away. All the people

disappeared. She was alone in a dark, quiet palace, seeing for the first time what she would really have in the long life ahead of her.

No one.

And she couldn't keep pretending that everything was fine as she had been doing all night.

Helia knew then what she had to do. It would take strength, but she had already proved to everyone—including herself—just how strong she was. She'd wanted to be there for Vasili, and she had been, but now it was time to choose herself.

Helia pulled herself back to the present. To the music and lights and people and took control.

'All good kings are territorial, are they not?' Helia said pleasantly. 'They have entire kingdoms to protect.'

Vasili's hand squeezed hers at her side.

'End of an era, then, I guess,' Stavros said, making a show of sliding his hands into his pockets. 'I would say you will be missed, but I'm greedy, so there's just more for us.'

'Have at it. I've grown tired of the scene anyway. I have more important things to concern myself with.'

'Enjoy the banquet,' Helia said, before any of them could say any more. 'If you'll excuse us?'

She walked hand in hand with Vasili through the room until she found Andreas.

'We will be leaving now,' she told him. 'Do what you need to.'

He looked between her and Vasili, nodded once, and set off.

It wasn't long after that when she was thanking everyone for attending and inviting them all to stay for as long as they liked. Vasili didn't challenge her as she took centre stage, all the while looking like a king who didn't bother himself with the opinions of anyone.

A lion in his den.

When they finally left, she kept silent until the door to their bedroom had clicked shut.

'Vasili, we need to talk.'

She watched him take a deep breath, then remove his sash and walk up to her. Gently, he removed the heavy crown from her head and took her hands in his.

'Helia, I want you to know how well you did tonight.'

'Thank you,' she said, and felt a crack forming within her as she steeled herself to say what she needed to.

She stepped away from his reach, knowing how weak she was for his touch. But not even that could stop her now.

'Thank you for allowing me to share in this life, Vasili, but it's time we faced reality.'

'What do you mean?'

He tried reaching for her again, but Helia shook her head and watched his hand drop.

'This life that we agreed to…it isn't going to work. For the kind of life you want to live, you don't need a queen.'

The words shattered the heart that she had exposed to him as if it was made of nothing but glass. Her vision was blurry, but she refused to cry.

'Helia—'

There was a flash of panic on his face that made it hard for her to speak, but she powered through it.

'I agreed to marry you for two reasons: the first being my need to help the orphanage, to help those who never get a chance to live the life Thalonia offers to its wealthy, the forgotten. And the second reason, Vasili, was you. I had admired you for so long, but those feelings paled in comparison to the way I felt seeing you with my people… how I feel about you now. But I realise that isn't enough.'

'Helia, you knew what this was,' Vasili said, his face a carefully blank mask.

'I did. But I also know that I deserve more than a lonely existence and a loveless marriage.' She stepped forward, placing her palm on his cheek. A single tear rolled down her own. 'You're a good man. A great king. And I know you'll see our project through.'

'Of course, I will. But Helia—'

'But nothing, Vasili. We both deserve more from this life, and I hope one day you will find it in you to let someone past your walls.'

Helia had known loving him would be a risk. She'd taken it anyway. And now, even though she tried to hold herself together, and even though she knew she was doing the right thing, her heart felt as if it was being ripped out of her chest.

'My advisors were right. You aren't an appropriate queen, because an appropriate queen wouldn't be good… like you. I wanted this to work.'

'So did I. Goodbye, Vasili.'

He held her gaze. Gritting his teeth.

Without a word, he turned around and left.

Helia waited until she heard the outer door close before she set herself into motion. Her heart in pieces, she could barely breathe through the agonising fracture carving through her.

She had to get out.

As quickly as she could, she gathered only the belongings that she would need and then left the King's quarters, slipping through the interconnecting door into a room she hadn't set foot in.

The unfamiliar surroundings were a small comfort.

There were no memories here. No hope. No laughter or stories shared. And that helped her keep control over her shattering emotions. Without much thought, she stepped under the shower, needing to wash Vasili's scent away. The memories would be punishment enough. She didn't need to smell him on herself as if he was beside her. He wouldn't be again.

With ruthless efficiency she scrubbed at her skin and her hair. Once she was done, she went in search of a bag, but she found only one. It would do. Helia stuffed her clothes in it, paying attention only to the next task and the next. It was the only way she could think around the pain in her chest.

She tied up her damp hair while instructing her chauffeur to meet her in the underground garage in the least conspicuous vehicle. She could hear the man's confusion, but he obeyed.

And then she was on the road. The black SUV with highly tinted windows was rolling through the gates and away from the palace.

Every atom in her wanted to look back. Wanted to look at the home she'd had with Vasili. Wanted to look for him.

Distance grew and it felt wrong. It was all wrong. They shouldn't be apart. But she needed to do this for herself. To give herself a chance at a happy life. She felt as though a thread was rapidly unspooling between them, going taut as they reached the end of the road and then snapping free completely when they turned the corner.

Helia covered her mouth to stifle the sob that bubbled up. She could no longer see the palace. She wouldn't see her husband again.

CHAPTER FIFTEEN

VASILI SQUINTED AWAKE. Bright sunlight fell across his bed through the open curtains, nearly blinding him. He rolled over, his hands on the cool sheets beside him. He had slept in his old room to give Helia space. Space that he'd hoped she would use to rethink her decision. She wanted to leave, and yet the days leading up to the coronation banquet had been perfect.

They'd kept to the agreement.

But now that very agreement might have cost him his queen.

She wouldn't have left in the night, he reasoned. Not with so many people in the palace. Perhaps he would be able to speak to Helia. Find a workable solution.

Throwing the covers off, he got out of bed and went about readying himself for this conversation. He didn't feel prepared for it, but it had to be done.

The palace was quiet when he stepped out of the room. So vastly different from the night before, with all the people, the music, the bright lights. It was as if a sombre hush had descended—but maybe that was a reflection of his own mood.

'Helia?' he called, knocking on the door to the room he had left her in the night before, but no answer came.

So he stepped inside and found everything exactly in its place.

Unease crept down his spine.

He opened the bedroom door and found the same. A bed that hadn't been slept in. There was no sign of her in the bathroom either. He rushed out of the room, moving towards the interconnecting door. Maybe she had needed to sleep elsewhere, just as he had. But again he found nothing in the sitting area. The only evidence of her was her discarded dress and the jewels on the bed.

Vasili rushed to the room she had used before she became Queen, feeling more desperate, more frantic with every passing second. And when he found no sign of life at all in that room, he pulled out his phone and called her.

'Damn it, Helia, pick up!'

But it went straight to voicemail.

It was obvious what had happened. He could feel it in his bones. In the silence.

Helia had left. She had said goodbye, and now she was gone.

He dropped onto the edge of the bed, his elbows on his knees, head hanging. If she didn't want to be reached he had to respect that, but it didn't stop the worry that was breaking him.

Was she okay? What if something happened to her?

She was the Queen. If anything had happened he would know. He told himself to hang on to that thought.

When she was ready, they would talk. When she was ready, he would lay out the terms of a new agreement.

Except he couldn't. He refused to be dictated to, but this time Helia had seized control. This time Helia had decided the terms, just as he had been doing before.

He curled his hands into fists. Of course she was un-happy. He had made her that way.

Vasili felt numb. Dead inside. As if a black hole had opened inside him, sucking away all the joy, all the happi-ness, leaving him empty. With a pounding headache.

'What have I done?' he whispered to the empty room.

Helia looked out of the window of the small mountain cabin. Filtered green-hued light poured into the modest lounge. Tall, lush trees stood on all sides of the little dwell-ing. There wasn't another person in sight. She was alone. As she had been for days.

The book she had been attempting to read for distrac-tion lay discarded on the coffee table. Instead, she stared out of the window with a cup of coffee warming her hands despite the heat of the day. A tear trickled down her cheek.

Once she'd been alone, she hadn't been able to stop them, and they still wouldn't abate. As if this pain was infinite. It had had a beginning, but there was certainly no end. She mourned the loss of Vasili. She'd loved him fiercely. She still did. She knew it had been a risk to fall in love with him. To show him that love without once telling him. But maybe now he would find the right person to share the bur-den of rule with. Someone he could keep at arm's length that his advisors would approve of.

The thought sent a fresh wave of tears down her face. It hurt more than she could bear to picture him with some-one else.

But she had seen them. Those women who were his equals.

They'd been at the banquet. Tall and polished in a way she would never manage. Maybe one of them would wear his ring...

She looked down at her finger, at the ring she still wore. At first it had been an oversight. In her hurry to leave, she hadn't even thought of it. But now, alone in this cabin, she couldn't bring herself to take it off. The last link to Vasili. She would have to return it eventually, but for now she curled her hand into her chest, replaying all the memories with him she held so close.

It would take a lifetime to get over Vasili—if she ever did. But she had to try. Because she couldn't be alone for the rest of her life. She had come to realise that she wanted children. She wanted love. And Vasili simply could not give that to her.

Helia spent that first week vacillating between hurt and anger. Vasili was one of the few people who could understand loneliness, but he was blind to hers. And now she had nothing. Not someone with whom to share a laugh or a knowing smile. She had lost everything. Her love, the career that she had worked so hard for, and her mission—although that had been achieved.

It was only in her second week of being holed up alone in the cabin that she felt she could breathe a little. As if she could pick herself up enough to restart her life. Could think through the pain. She needed to get her career back on track, but it couldn't be in Thalonia. Not when she had briefly been its queen. She would have to find a new home.

Her heart broke for yet another reason. This love had indeed cost her everything—including her home.

Hollow. That was what Vasili was. What his days were. Robotic. Mechanical. Vasili went through the motions every day. Eat. Barely sleep. Work.

It had been two weeks. Two weeks of hell. Two weeks of feeling bereft. Broken. The palace seemed even colder since

Helia left. Emptier. Everyone avoided him when they could. He didn't have it in him to make small talk or exchange pleasantries. There was nothing to be pleasant about. So he threw himself into his duties instead. Or tried to.

As Vasili sat behind his desk he heard the door open, followed by the sound of Andreas taking his seat for their meeting. But he couldn't concentrate on the task at hand. There wasn't anything in his life that didn't remind him of Helia. Of her words before she left.

She was right—she deserved more than a life of loneliness. Wasn't that what he wanted? Why he had tried to be in her corner? Because he knew loneliness. Except now it was dawning on him that maybe it was his own fear that had allowed his loneliness to persevere. It was his fear of being hurt that had had him erecting barriers around himself.

For a shining moment on their honeymoon he had known what it felt like to have someone care about him. To have support at his back. And what had he done? He'd pushed Helia away the night she'd offered to give him the space to grieve.

And he'd kept pushing her away.

Every single day he'd enjoyed being around her. Wanted her and cared for her. Every day he'd enjoyed her wit and affection and consideration. And in return he'd given her nothing but empty touches.

Except they hadn't really been empty, had they? He'd had to fight his feelings for her. He'd made that rule not to be intimate to protect himself.

Vasili had had to fight hard to ensure he didn't grow attached to his wife. The last time he'd trusted his heart to someone in any kind of bond he'd been fifteen, and Sophia had been forced to leave. When he and Leander had finally been free to nurture a brotherly bond, he'd been killed.

When he had allowed himself to be with Helia she'd got under his skin, but he had feared that it would only be a matter of time before she too found a reason to leave.

Vasili had been happy to have sex with Helia, for them to appear as a king and queen should, but he had refused to love her—and didn't that make him like his parents?

A throat was cleared. 'Your Majesty...?'

Vasili didn't register the interruption. Not now he'd realised how much fear had ruled his life.

He'd walled off his heart for fear of being hurt like he had been by his parents. He'd kept Helia away when he was grieving his brother because it had hurt to lose Leander. How could he let in another person who would hurt him? That was all he'd known.

But with Helia he had been happy. Relaxed. Less alone. Helia had taken his grief and made it bearable.

He thought back to that morning on the beach, when he'd seen her grief. While he'd taught her to swim, it hadn't been just lust burning through his veins—it had been so much more. It had been finding someone who understood.

'I hope one day you will find it in you to let someone in past your walls.'

He already had. But he hadn't had to let her in—she'd burrowed through with her love and care. She had seen him. Vasili. Not a royal or a son who wasn't worthy.

'Sir...' Andreas said as he quietly closed the binder on Vasili's desk. 'Go to her. Bring her back.'

'I can't do that, Andreas.'

Vasili closed his own folders. He couldn't see anything in them anyway.

'You know, there have been many things I have disagreed with you on,' said Andreas. 'But throughout your rebellions and your disregard of our traditions, none of your sins has been as egregious as this.'

'Watch yourself, Andreas. I'm willing to take your advice, but you are very close to overstepping,' Vasili growled.

'I may have my own thoughts on your queen, but neither of you deserves this—and the Kingdom doesn't deserve a king lost in misery.'

'If I didn't know better, I'd say you miss her,' said Vasili.

'Perhaps I do.' Andreas stopped at the door. 'I am a traditionalist, but my concern had always been for what is best for the throne. And in the end, even if we disagreed, Queen Helia proved those concerns unwarranted. You're not the only one who's had time to think.'

Vasili scrubbed his hands down his face when the door softly clicked shut. Yanking on his desk drawer, to store away the files on his table, he saw an envelope slide forward.

His father's letter.

He picked it up and closed the drawer, turning it over in his hand. He was already in torment—what was a little more? If there was ever a time to read the words of a man who had never cared for much, it was now.

Vasili pulled the letter free and unfolded it, seeing the familiar scrawl. He could almost picture his father with his black fountain pen in hand.

He began to read…

My dearest Vasili,
How I wish you'd never have to read this letter…

Of course he had—because if everything had gone to plan, Leander would have been in this chair.

…I know you will read those words and think I have written this because I never wished for you to be King, and that is my own fault, but the truth is that

I wish you still had your brother. That you did not have to be alone.

I mentioned this in my previous letter, but I fear, even as I write that you may not have read the words and that is undoubtedly my fault.

I have many regrets in life, Vasili, but perhaps you are my greatest. I regret that I put the crown before you. I saw every day what my choice did to you. You see, I was deluded into thinking that this throne was the most important thing. That everything else was secondary. Including my family. Including anything as frivolous as happiness. That withholding affection and raising you both to put duty first would create strong leaders. Kings.

I don't want you to make the same mistakes, Vasili. Learn from mine. Do not repeat them and become like me, an old man on his deathbed seeing with clarity for the first time and filled with regret.

You are strong, son. Perhaps the strongest of us all. You stood up for yourself, for what you wanted and believed in. As much as it irritated me, I admired you for it so much more. This is how I know you will be a strong king. A good king.

This throne is a lonely place, son, so find yourself a queen who will not just be what Thalonia needs, but what you need first.

I'm sorry I didn't tell you this enough, and I'm sorry it comes in two letters, but I love you, Vasili. I would stand over your crib every night and marvel at just how much it was possible to love something so little and so precious.

I know it is too late to say all of this, but I am sorry, son.

I love you and believe in you.

With regret for destroying the first letter his father had left him roiling in his belly, Vasili read through this one to his father's signed-off scrawl and then tossed it aside. He propped his elbows on the table, resting his forehead against his laced fingers.

He could have read those words that he'd so wanted to hear a year ago. Could have known he had been loved. And it was his own fault that he hadn't, because he'd been so hurt and angry.

There was so much hurt in his family. That was their true legacy. Vasili couldn't even find it in himself to be angry any more. A letter did not make up for twenty-nine years of rejection, but it did show him a man lost in his misery. In the wrong choices.

Just as he had made the wrong choices.

Vasili had the perfect queen and he realised that he loved her with a viciousness. She was exactly what he needed. She had been from the start.

So now he sat at a crossroads. He could wallow in all that he had lost and wall his heart off permanently—because no one would touch it as Helia had—and then he would become yet another soulless king. Or he could fight the fear. Find the bravery he had been blessed with to rebel, but use it to go after the woman he loved. The woman who loved him back. Who had changed his life.

And just like at the start of all this madness, there was no real choice. Because the only right answer was to choose Helia.

CHAPTER SIXTEEN

VASILI STOOD AT the door to a modest cabin nestled amongst tall dark trees. Though he could hear the sea, he couldn't see it. He looked over his shoulder at the path he had driven up. The blacked-out SUV looked almost garish in the serene forest.

So much oppressive, insulating greenness.

Helia had retreated and it was his fault, but he would make it right. He had to.

Vasili knocked, and sent up a silent prayer that she would listen.

The door swung open and there she was. In jeans, with her hair piled messily on top of her head, without a scrap of make-up, and she was by far the most beautiful thing he had ever seen.

Vasili finally breathed a breath that didn't feel as though it had been forced through a fissure in his chest.

'Hello, Helia,' he said.

'Vasili…' Shock rippled across her face. 'What are you doing here?'

'May I come in?'

He could see the doubt within her. And, as much as it hurt, he didn't blame her for being uneasy about letting him in.

'Please. I just want to talk.'

He watched her take a breath and stand aside, allowing him to pass through the door. From the entrance hall he could see the sitting area, the kitchen and the dining table. A glaring reminder of Helia's past life and how different it was from his.

And against the wall was a packed bag.

'Join me?' he asked as he took a seat at the table.

It was a reminder of a different time when he had asked the same of her. Except then he had laid down the rules and expected Helia to follow. Now he would give her the choice.

'I don't know if that's a good idea, Vasili. I don't know why you're here, but there isn't much left to say.'

'There's plenty to say. Starting with I'm sorry.'

Helia scrunched up her eyes, wrapping her arms around herself as if she needed protection from him, and it made Vasili furious with himself.

'Please don't. It's not going to change anything.'

'That's where you're wrong. Everything has changed. Let me explain, Helia. I beg you.'

He could hear the rawness in his own voice and wondered if it was his obvious brokenness that convinced Helia to join him at the table. Close enough to touch. But he would not do that until she allowed him to.

His eyes drifted to the bag. 'Are you going somewhere?'

'I'm leaving Thalonia. There's nothing here for me. I need a new start.'

That was the last thing he wanted to hear. Thalonia needed her. *He* needed her. He wouldn't let her leave without a fight.

'How did you find me?' she asked softly. 'I left instructions not to tell you where I was.'

'I know. That's why I paid a visit to Giannis Demetriou.'

Vasili slid an envelope over to Helia and placed a vibrantly purple iris on top of it.

'What is this?'

He heard her voice catch as her eyes filled with tears.

'That, Helia, is every cent of your inheritance. The start in life your father left you. After we're done here today, if you still wish to leave, it will help you. As will I. I'm not going to abandon you.'

'I don't know what to say...'

'Then let me start.'

Vasili could bear it no more and reached for her hand. The spark of her touch restarted his heart, which had grown cold and empty without her. He took a deep breath, trying to find the words. The only thing he could tell her was the truth, but he needed to start somewhere. He needed to lay himself bare to this woman, which was a terrifying thought, but there was no longer room in his life for fear.

'I was scared. I have been afraid for a very long time. Afraid to expose my heart to anyone. I've come to realise it was I who kept Leander away, not the other way round. He tried, but I wouldn't get close. Not when I had been warned away. But I was wrong. I loved my brother a great deal, and I see that now. I also see how grieving him only made me want to wall myself off further.'

Vasili let out a shuddering breath. Felt his throat closing up with the ache of his loss. Helia said nothing, but the squeeze of her hand was support enough.

'I wanted my parents to love me, and when they didn't— or appeared not to—it hurt. But I had Sophia. And then, when she was gone, there was nothing to stop me pushing everyone away. It's why I didn't love anyone. It's why I never had true friends. And it's why I tried to keep you at arm's length. Because you, Helia…you were a danger to me from the start.'

'Me?'

'That day in the library I was lost to my grief. Drowning in it. In my anger at what was being asked of me. My mind was loud, roaring with frustration, with the injustice of it all. But then I looked at you, and for a moment it was peaceful. And when I kissed you, I was lost in it. Moved in a way I had never been. And I knew if you had that power with a simple kiss, you had the power to destroy me. I couldn't let that happen. So I selfishly chose myself over you and I hurt you. I'm so sorry.'

'Why are you telling me this?'

Helia's voice was rough through her tears. Tears he knew weren't just for herself, but because of his own anguish.

'You were so brave to stand up to the King and Queen from such a young age, Vasili, and yet you were a coward when that rebellion led to something real and powerful.'

She was right. He had been a coward. Even though it had been a fight not to fall in love with her, he had done so anyway. And still he'd tried to keep her away from his heart. There was no bravery there.

'I was. And it took you walking out for me to realise what a fearful idiot I have been. You took control. And because of you I can see things so much clearer. Because of you I can finally own up to my feelings. That morning when I woke up and realised you had left…'

Vasili swallowed hard. Swallowed down those feelings that now returned. Anger at himself. Hopelessness. His eyes had been opened that day.

'It broke me. In trying to keep you from destroying me, I'd made it happen.'

'So why are you here now? What do you want?'

'I want you back. I want you in my bed. I want you in my life. I want to change this kingdom with you! I love you, Helia. I love you so goddamn much that I ache with it.'

There they were. The words Helia had longed to hear. And they made her want to run into his arms and stay there for ever.

But his admitting the truth didn't change their situation. Would he still want to end the monarchy, which meant she would never have a family? Was he prepared for the kind of life she wanted?

'I have waited for those words, Vasili. There was something about you even when I didn't know you that drew me in, and when I did get to know you I couldn't help but fall in love with you. But loving each other isn't enough. I need to know what's different now.'

It took a moment for him to respond.

'In my mind, if the people meant to care for me couldn't, how could I be worthy of it from anyone else? From you? But here's the thing… I know I used that as a shield. It came from fear, and I have no room in my life for fear any more. That's what's different. I'm done with shields. With keeping everyone away.'

'But we want different things. I can't return with you now only to have my heart broken later.'

She'd had the strength to leave once, but it had gouged at her soul to do so. She didn't want to do it again. She couldn't. Just thinking about it nearly paralysed her.

'Tell me what you want and it's yours. Anything.'

She could hear the desperation in his voice.

'I want a family. I want children, and a husband who isn't afraid to give me his whole heart. I don't want to be lonely any more.'

Her voice broke on that last word. Her stomach dropped as the chair scraped loudly against the floor as Vasili dragged her to him and cradled her face.

'You have my heart. My soul. And with time we could have a family.'

Helia tried to pull away. 'Don't feed me false hope. We both know how you feel about children.'

'You know, I believe I still owe you a thought,' he said, not letting her go.

Their honeymoon seemed as if it had been eons ago, but she would never forget that night she'd offered to leave. When he'd said he didn't want her to go.

'I dreamt of it once,' he said. 'Our children…with curly hair and your smile. I craved it but I pushed it aside, thinking that life wasn't for me. I was so convinced I knew what would happen to my children that I wanted no part of it. But then I read a letter my father had left in Leander's care, to be given to me in the event of my brother's death, and I know now that he loved me. He chose not to show it, because that's what he thought he needed to do in order to be a good king. I have said it before. I am not my father and I believe that now. I have made different choices. And that life I dreamt of with you… I want that too.'

Helia could see the sincerity in Vasili's eyes. It made what was left of her resistance crumble, because the picture of life he'd painted was exactly what she was leaving Thalonia to find.

'I hate it that you didn't get the love you needed growing up. I hate it that your parents made such awfully bad choices. And I especially hate it that those choices made you believe that you weren't worthy of love. That they made you stop loving yourself. But you need to know I will always love you. No matter what happens. I will always be yours, and I know that your people love you, Vasili.'

'Helia…' he whispered brokenly.

'Do you know what I saw after our wedding? Happiness. I saw smiles on every face in the crowd. They were happy for you. Happy to have you as their king. The man who treated everyone in his palace with kindness. You think I didn't notice the way you spoke to everyone? You think that was a secret or overlooked? It wasn't. I paid attention. I saw what you didn't.'

He leaned his forehead against hers. 'I wish that I'd met you sooner.'

'Then tell me you want me. Tell me it's not a mistake for me to go back with you. That you won't get scared again and push me away.'

Because Helia wanted to go with him. As much as she was hoping for the life she deserved, she knew there was only ever one man she would love like this. Only one man who would ever make her heart pound and set her blood ablaze. Her eyes fell on the envelope. Only one man who had ever fought for her. And after these two weeks of constant heartache and never-ending tears, in Vasili's embrace she felt hopeful. Lighter. Happy. As if a light had been turned back on.

'I want you,' he said. 'I want you every day. I want you when you're cranky in the mornings, and I want you in my arms at night. I want you for the rest of our lives and then some. You're it for me, Helia. I promise that I will never push you away and that you will never know another day of loneliness. Neither of us will.'

'Then give me your ring.'

Without hesitation, Vasili handed his gold wedding band to Helia, who gave him hers.

Taking his hand, she said, 'Vasili, I promise to love you every day. I promise to remind you to love yourself when you forget, and to love you harder when you can't. I promise to be the friend you deserve and the partner you can count on. I promise to always be honest with you, and I promise I will never be taken from you.'

She watched his eyes glisten as she slid his ring back onto his finger. These vows were so different from those they'd made last time. There were no secret messages or hidden feelings. These words felt sacred. This union was divine.

'Helia, I have a lot to work on, and I promise to work on being better, on being the man you deserve. It might take a while…' he smiled when she laughed '…but we will get there.' He twirled the ring in the sunlight. 'Maybe I always knew it would be you. Maybe I was fighting a truth that already existed. You and I—we're inevitable. And here is your proof.'

Helia looked down at the ring he held, noticing for the first time the Latin phrase engraved on the inside of the thin band.

'It means *My salvation…my eternal.*'

'Vasili…' Helia breathed.

Tears ran down her cheeks and he brushed them away with the backs of his fingers.

'That's what you are, and I promise to show you as much every single day.'

Vasili slid the ring onto her finger and then, in a crash of limbs and bodies and lips, they kissed. They kissed without restraint. They kissed as if they had been reunited after an eternity apart. And they kissed as if this was their start.

'Well, then, Your Majesty,' Helia said as she pushed the

envelope back to him. 'I believe this should go to the orphanage. The Queen has little need of it.'

'As you wish.' He smiled. Bright and glorious. 'Let's go home.'

And it felt right. As if a part of her soul had healed. For Helia had found her home. It was here, in the arms of her husband. A man she loved so much. And now that love didn't make her feel alone—instead it made her stronger and more hopeful and blissfully happy.

EPILOGUE

Six years later

VASILI STOOD BETWEEN the two little beds and as quietly and gently as he could tucked the covers around one little girl and then the other.

His daughters. Neither of whom resembled him nor Helia.

Two years after they'd married, Vasili and Helia had made the decision to break with tradition yet again and adopted their first child. A beautiful two-year-old girl. Eighteen months later, they'd adopted their second.

At first, he had been terrified he wouldn't be a good father. That he would repeat the mistakes of his own. But with he and Helia being so closely involved with the orphanage, Vasili knew he loved the children in a way he hadn't been.

He had come to the realisation that it wasn't the throne that he was angry with—it was his parents. The crown had the power to help, to better people's lives, as he and Helia had been doing. All the orphanages were well looked after and well-funded. With the King and Queen involved, they were no longer hopeless places. Children like Helia had been were no longer forgotten. The country's schools were thriving, and all children were able to study without

the worry of expense thanks to the Leander Leos Founda-
tion. Even the tax bill had been amended with little fight,
and Thalonia was thriving.

The truth he'd had to accept was that the crown wasn't
responsible for the lack of affection he'd experienced. Their
treatment of 'the spare' had been his parents' choice, and he
chose to love *his* children demonstrably. Though one of his
children would inevitably become the monarch one day—
the first in Thalonia's history not to be royal by blood—
none of them would be treated as the heir or spare. Those
words were never uttered in the palace.

He'd made peace with the fact that he didn't need to end
the monarchy. He just needed to make it better.

He needed to be a better king than the ones before him.
A better husband. A better father.

Vasili had kept his father's letter. Had read through it frequently to remind himself of what the wrong choices meant.
How love could be hidden and lost because of them. That
letter wasn't a punishment he inflicted upon himself. It was,
instead, the greatest lesson his father could have imparted,
and the reason Vasili had come to forgive the late King.

Together, Vasili and Helia put the girls to bed every
night. Though he would always come back in for just a
little while longer. It was overwhelming just how much he
loved them. His family.

He turned on the night light and made his way to the
bedroom, where his wife waited.

Helia…

She was every bit as beautiful to him now as she had
been the first day he saw her. She tugged back the covers
in silent invitation. One hand rested on her belly, swollen
with the son they would soon welcome, the other was holding the duvet.

'I take it they're still asleep?' She smiled knowingly.

He laughed. 'They are.'

'Good. But now, Your Majesty, your wife requires your attention.'

And he was happy to give it.

Vasili had never envisaged a life as perfect as this. Hadn't dared to dream of it. But as he pulled his wife into his arms, and kissed her with a burning passion, he was glad he hadn't.

Because no dream could compare with this Elysian reality.

* * * * *

HARLEQUIN
Reader Service

Enjoyed your book?

Try the perfect subscription for Romance readers and get more great books like this delivered right to your door.

See why over 10+ million readers have tried Harlequin Reader Service.

Start with a Free Welcome Collection with free books and a gift—valued over $20.

Choose any series in print or ebook. See website for details and order today:

TryReaderService.com/subscriptions